Seducing the S

By

Diana Bold

This is a work of fiction. Names, characters, places, and incidents are products of the author's imagination or are used fictitiously and are not to be construed as real. Any resemblance to actual events, locales, organizations, or persons, living or dead, is entirely coincidental.

Seducing the Spinster

By Diana Bold

Cover Artist: Amanda Koehler Designs

Author's Note

Because Julian and Jane's story is so intertwined with Michael and Emma's from MARRYING THE AMERICAN HEIRESS, I've had to include a few of the conversations that all four characters were a part of, though they are told from a different POV in this book. So if you feel like you've read some of this before, you're not imagining it. I hope you enjoy seeing those scenes through Julian and Jane's eyes.

Prologue

Basingstoke Castle – February 1860

Julian Tremaine, the Earl of Basingstoke, crushed Lady Jane Bennett's hastily scrawled note in his fist as he strode quickly through the wooded hills that separated his own country estate from that of Jane's father, the Marquess of Langston. He couldn't imagine what had prompted her to send for him. Jane had never been given to dramatics, so he knew something must be terribly wrong.

Meet me at our special place, she'd written. *I need you.*

Though less than a mile separated his property from hers, the walk through the trees seemed to take forever, the chill wind cutting through him like a knife as his mind raced with the possibilities. When he finally crested the hill above the small hunting cottage where he and Jane had shared their first kiss just six short months ago, he found her waiting for him out front, the weak winter sun catching in her golden hair. Even from this distance, he could tell that she was crying.

His heart seized in his chest, and he stumbled to a stop. Her tears reminded him of his mother, sobbing in her bed after the deaths of his older brother and younger sister. All of his subsequent memories of her had been filled with her tears, until she'd finally joined his siblings, dying of what he'd always been convinced was a broken heart. A woman's tears had wrecked him ever since.

Jane had always been so sunny and bright. In fact, that was probably what drew him to her, why he loved her so deeply. She represented happiness for him, and since his life sometimes seemed to be just one tragedy after another, he desperately needed that.

For one cowardly moment, he wanted nothing more than to turn and run back the way he had come, completely uncertain of his ability to give her the comfort she so obviously needed. Shaking himself, ashamed that he'd allowed such a thought to cross his mind, he ran toward her instead, sweeping her up against him in a tight embrace.

"Jane," he murmured into her lavender-scented hair, finding comfort of his own in the feel of her body pressed to his. "What's wrong? Why are you crying, sweetheart?"

She shook her head against his chest, sobbing even harder now. "It's... my father..." she managed at last.

"Your father?" he asked, cupping her chin and lifting her face, staring down into her lovely tear-streaked face. Her blue eyes were puffy and swollen, as though she'd been crying for days. "What happened to your father?"

Her eyes welled with fresh tears. "He's... gone." Her bottom lip trembled. "Oh, Julian. He didn't come down for breakfast.... And when... his valet tried to wake him..."

"Ah, Jane... I'm so sorry." He hugged her even tighter, knowing all too well how it felt to lose a parent. His mother had died five years ago, and his father had drunk himself to death only a few years later. In all, he'd lost four of the five members of his immediate family in less than three years. Only his younger brother, Ethan, remained.

Jane had also lost her mother, and she'd never had any siblings, so she had no one now.

No one but me.

As he pressed his face to hers, he felt how chilled she was. Though the sun was shining, the day was bitterly cold, which seemed rather fitting, given what he'd just learned. Sweeping her up in his arms, he strode toward the cottage, kicking open the door and depositing her in the center of the small bed in the corner. Before she could protest, he tucked several rough woolen blankets around her.

"Stay there," he murmured. "I'm going to start a fire."

He turned away, busying himself at the fireplace for several minutes as he got a small fire burning in the hearth. His mind raced as he forced himself to acknowledge Jane's new circumstances. She'd just turned eighteen, and they'd always been expected to marry. Now that her father was gone, he didn't know what she'd do, or where she'd go. He had a feeling that her father's estate would be deeply in debt, given the fact that the man had a gambling problem and had been burning through his fortune for years now. The closest male relation, who was but a distant cousin, would inherit the estate, and Jane would be at his mercy.

The obvious solution would be to officially propose. Then, after her mourning period was over, they could wed, and he'd give her the protection of his wealth and name.

Panic surged through him. He loved Jane. She was his very best friend, and she'd helped him through his own father's death. He wanted to marry her. Truly, he did. But he was only twenty. He'd just inherited an earldom. He wasn't sure he was ready to take on yet another responsibility.

Sighing, he turned back to the bed and crawled beneath the blankets, pulling Jane into his arms. "I'm here," he murmured, brushing a few strands of silky golden hair from her face. "I'm here for you, Jane."

"Thank you," she whispered, snuggling her face against his chest, her small body shivering uncontrollably. "I shouldn't have run away from the house. But... I couldn't bear to be there with him... when he was gone. And... I wanted you. I knew you'd come. I can always count on you."

"Of course," he assured her, her words making him feel even worse about the doubts churning within him. "I'll always be here for you, Jane. Always."

But her father's death changed everything. Their relationship had always been a bit one-sided, with her being the one to give him comfort as he tried to work through his own grief and his anger at his brother Ethan, who he sometimes blamed for it all. Could he help her the way she'd helped him?

Even now, he knew he shouldn't be here like this with her. It went against everything society deemed proper. If they were caught alone together, despite the extenuating circumstances, her reputation would be ruined, and he'd be forced to marry her.

Why was that idea suddenly so terrifying?

Perhaps, deep down, he knew that he didn't deserve her. She was too good for him, too sweet and perfect to be forever saddled with his darkness. He should let her go to London, have a Season, and find someone who would be better suited to her.

His arms tightened around her at the very thought. Even if he didn't deserve her, she was his. It would kill him to see her with someone else.

For half an hour more, he held her, whispering inane platitudes and gently rubbing her slim back in an effort to soothe her pain. At last, her sobs subsided, and she lay passively in his embrace, completely hollowed out by the depth of her sorrow.

"I should go back," she whispered, her voice hoarse and raw. "There's so much that needs to be done."

He hugged her tight, then reluctantly let her go. "I'll go with you. I'll help."

She stared at him with those beautiful teary eyes, and the trust and love he saw there made him feel even more guilt and doubt. He wasn't worthy of so much love. He knew that he'd eventually disappoint her.

JANE HELD JULIAN'S letter in her trembling hands, tears streaking her cheeks as she forced herself to read it one more time.

Dear Jane,

I've been called away to London. I won't be there for your father's burial. Know that my thoughts and prayers will be with you.

I'm so sorry.

Julian

She kept thinking she was missing something, that she'd somehow misinterpreted what he'd said. Only yesterday, he'd held her so tenderly and promised he'd be there for her no matter what.

What could be so important that he'd leave her when she needed him most? Her first thought had been to worry for him, to hope something hadn't happened to Ethan, the only family member he had left, but in her heart, she knew that wasn't true.

He'd run away.

Though he'd stood by her side all day yesterday, she'd sensed the restlessness in him, the fear. He'd said and done all the right things, but there had been something cornered and rebellious in his gaze. As though her father's death had stripped him of his choices. She knew he felt as though he had to marry her now, and that obviously terrified him.

Why? He was her best friend, the one person she'd always felt understood her. Their relationship had been so simple, so precious. She couldn't help but feel hurt and betrayed by his actions. She wasn't trying to pressure him into marriage. She just wanted him to be here for her while she laid her father to rest. Was that too much to ask?

A sudden surge of fury consumed her, and she ripped the letter to shreds, letting the pieces fall to the floor. Her father was gone, and the creditors were already nipping at her heels. A distant cousin was set to take the title and everything that had been entailed. All she'd have left was the London townhouse, but she knew her father hadn't left her enough money to maintain it for long. Before his death, the marquess had gambled away most of his fortune, including her dowry, always convinced that he'd win it all back. If not for a small inheritance from her maternal grandmother, she wouldn't make it through the year without having to impose upon some friend or distant family member to take her in. She could probably go stay with the Duke of Clayton, her mother's brother, and be a companion to her cousin Natalia, but though she and Natalia were close, she would hate that. The last thing she wanted was to be a burden.

She'd thought she could count on Julian, but it was becoming clearer to her by the moment that the only person she could count on was herself.

Straightening her shoulders, she dried her angry tears and lifted her chin. Somehow, she'd find her own way, no matter what that entailed. And above all else, she promised herself to never believe in a man again.

Chapter One

Seven Years Later
London – June 1867

"Let's get this over with."

Julian grinned at his friend Michael Blake's grim pronouncement. "Those aren't the words one usually uses when they are about to meet their future bride."

Michael glared at him as they strode through the theater, on their way to a private box that held Julian's old friend, Lady Jane Bennett, and her companion, Miss Emma Marks. "I'm not in the mood to be teased about this."

Julian tried to hold back his mirth because he knew just how badly Michael dreaded meeting Miss Marks, the American heiress who was the key to his family's financial difficulties. However, he'd always enjoyed poking fun at his straight-laced friend. "You never know. You might actually like her. You should at least give her a chance before you fall into despair."

Michael sighed and swept an errant strand of blond hair out of his eyes. "Sorry. I suppose you're right. I just hate being backed into a corner like this."

Julian gave him a sympathetic glance. Despite his amusement, he felt a bit cornered as well. He hadn't seen Jane

Bennett in seven years—not since he'd walked out on her after her father's death. In fact, he hadn't even known she was in London until Michael had asked for an introduction earlier this evening.

Michael had remembered that Julian's country estate had bordered Jane's father's, and he'd thought Julian the perfect person to arrange his first meeting with Miss Marks. Julian had to admit that the prospect of speaking with Jane again both thrilled and terrified him. He was trying to act supremely confident about the matter, but he had no idea how Jane would react to him after all these years. He'd treated her so poorly...

No, if he were being honest with himself, he had to admit that his actions had been worse than deplorable. He'd broken her heart. He'd held her that first day, when her grief over her father's death had been fresh and traumatic, but the next morning, he'd made an excuse to go to London, where he'd lost himself in drinking and whoring, trying to forget how much he'd disappointed her.

Weeks had passed, and one morning he'd woken with a pounding headache and a heart full of regret. He'd stayed away too long, and he'd known nothing he could say at this late date could make up for what he'd done. He'd failed her so terribly that it was much easier to stay in London and pretend she'd never meant anything to him. In fact, after a few years, he managed to put all thoughts of her away and convince himself that she was simply the first of the many women who would come in and out of his life. He'd comforted himself with the thought that she'd surely wed a staid country lord and was happy and content raising children and dogs in some country pile, having forgotten all about him.

But in all the years since, he'd never felt so comfortable, so much himself, around any other woman. He'd known none of the women who graced his bed actually cared about him. They simply liked the things he could give them—the power of his wealth and rank.

As if all of this wasn't bad enough, Michael had also revealed that Jane was apparently sponsoring the American girl, allowing Miss Marks to live in her Mayfair home while she introduced her to society. Rumor had it that she was being paid handsomely for this service. He hated to hear that she'd been reduced to such dire straits. She was the daughter of a marquess, for God's sake! Why hadn't she married? Even though her father had gambled away her dowry, he'd assumed someone else would be thrilled to make her his bride.

He took a deep breath, shaking his head to clear it of his riotous thoughts, then stopped before the footman who stood on their side of the heavy velvet partition. "Please tell Lady Jane that Lord Basingstoke would like to speak with her."

However, before the man could announce them, Jane swept back the curtain. Her eyes widened, and her face went blank when she saw who stood on the other side. "Lord Basingstoke," she said, her voice utterly emotionless. "What are you doing here?"

Julian met her direct blue gaze, and something deep inside him, something he'd thought long dead, came roaring back to life. She still had the power to take his breath away, something he hadn't anticipated. "Good evening, Lady Jane. I've come to arrange an introduction between my friend Lord Sherbourne and your lovely companion Miss Marks."

Jane recovered quickly from her surprise. Whatever she might feel about seeing Julian after all these years, she was keeping it to herself. She stood slightly aside and gestured behind her. "Lord Basingstoke, Lord Sherbourne, may I present Miss Emma Marks of New York City?"

"It's a pleasure to meet you, my lords." The dark-haired beauty behind Jane stood and curtsied gracefully. Julian didn't know what Michael was so worried about. The girl had perfect manners.

Sherbourne stepped forward in resignation. "The pleasure is mine," he murmured, his voice clipped. Taking her gloved hand, he brought it briefly to his lips. Then he stepped back, and an awkward silence fell upon the group.

Wincing inwardly at his friend's deplorable lack of charm, Julian smiled at the heiress, determined to smooth things over and save Michael from himself. "Are you enjoying your visit, Miss Marks?"

"I'm enjoying London very much," she responded brightly, obviously as determined as he to make polite conversation.

"I hear you're quite the world traveler." Though Julian continued speaking to Miss Marks, he stared at Jane out of the corner of his eye, wishing she'd look at him, give him some clue how she was feeling. "Tell us about your journeys. Have you been anywhere fascinating and exotic?"

"I've traveled extensively on the Continent during the past two years. I must admit, however, to being a bit of a history enthusiast, the older and dustier the better. I'd love to visit Egypt, but I haven't yet had the chance." Miss Marks' enthusiasm for the subject was clear, and Julian suddenly felt more confident about the possibility of a match between Miss Marks and Michael.

"What a coincidence." Julian glanced quickly at Michael, hoping he'd jump on the topic. "Sherbourne is an amateur archaeologist. He's fascinated by all things Egyptian. In fact, he's sponsored several expeditions and has an amazing collection of artifacts."

Emma turned to Michael, sudden excitement sparkling in her eyes. "Have you been to Egypt, Lord Sherbourne? Have you seen the great pyramids and the Sphinx?"

"I've never left England," Michael admitted, and Julian knew how much the fact pained his friend, who had an adventurous streak he'd never been allowed to indulge. "My responsibilities don't allow for frivolities such as travel."

Though she obviously understood that he'd meant to rebuke her, Emma smiled. "Well, no wonder you collect Egyptian artifacts. Everyone needs a little something exotic in their lives. I'd love to see your collection."

Jane gasped audibly at Emma's forward behavior, but Julian merely chuckled and gave her a covert wink. He liked this girl.

Michael looked slightly stunned, as though he had no idea what to make of her. "I keep my artifacts in the country, at Sherbourne Hall, but perhaps something can be arranged." He took a deep breath, as though girding himself for something unpleasant. "In the meantime, would you allow me to call on you? At your earliest convenience?"

"Of course, you may call upon me," Miss Marks replied graciously. "I'd be delighted."

"Excellent. You may expect me tomorrow morning." Bowing stiffly, Sherbourne turned and left their box.

Julian smiled and shrugged. "What can I say, Miss Marks? He's an acquired taste." Hoping Michael hadn't ruined his chances with the heiress, he finally turned his entire attention to Jane "It was a pleasure to see you again, Lady Jane. You've been absent from Society for far too long."

Jane stared at him without comment, still unruffled, giving nothing of her feelings away.

He met her gaze for a long moment, remembering the trick he had up his sleeve, surprisingly happy to be in her sweet, calming presence again after so long apart.

Why didn't I stay for her father's funeral? She needed me, and I failed her. I can't believe she isn't ordering me to leave.

Determined to keep things light, he laughed and produced a single red rose with a quick flick of his wrist. His older brother Nathanial had taught him the trick before he'd died, and for some reason, tonight he'd hidden the rose in his jacket with the intention of performing it for some lovely lady. He'd just never expected that lady to be Jane.

"Oh, Julian." Jane's mask finally fell, and she accepted the rose, sudden tears filling her eyes. "It's beautiful."

He stared down at her, wanting to tell her that she was lovelier than any rose could ever be, but he knew he'd lost his chance to whisper sweet words to her. Suddenly, he regretted the rose trick. This was Jane. She wasn't like all his other conquests, not merely a game to be won. In fact, she was the only woman he'd ever loved. And as he gazed into her blue eyes, he wondered if he'd ever really gotten over her. Swallowing thickly, he whirled and left the box.

His mind racing and heart aching, he hurried after Michael, who seemed determined to leave the theater entirely.

Bloody hell. He'd never expected seeing Jane again to resurrect all those old feelings for her he'd thought long dead. But now that he'd seen her, now that he knew what had happened to her, how could he possibly ignore the fact that he was largely to blame for her reduced circumstances? She should have been his wife...

He finally caught up to Michael on the bustling street outside. "I don't know what all the fuss is about," he commented, hoping to take his mind off of Jane. "I find Miss Marks quite refreshing."

Michael threw him an exasperated glance. "If you like her so much, why don't *you* marry her?"

Julian chuckled openly. "Because I don't need her dowry, my friend. And I haven't any relatives breathing down my neck, insisting I breed an heir. Besides, if I married her, what would you do? There aren't any other heiresses of her ilk this season."

"I'm aware of that. Otherwise, I certainly wouldn't be considering an American," Michael snapped.

"American or not, she's one of the most exotically beautiful creatures I've ever seen." Julian raised one brow. "Don't tell me you didn't notice."

"I prefer my women blonde and biddable," Michael replied, still angry.

"Blonde and biddable?" Julian scoffed. "You'd be bored to death in a month." He shook his head. "If you ask me, I think your brother has the right idea. I don't intend to wed until I find someone who makes me feel the way Dylan feels about Lady Natalia."

Michael gave him a disbelieving glance as Julian motioned for his driver to bring up the coach. "You can't mean never to marry. What about your title? Surely, you don't want your wastrel of a brother to inherit it?"

"I don't give a damn about my title," Julian replied bitterly. "It's brought me nothing but misfortune. Ethan is welcome to it, though I doubt he'd want it either."

Julian's luxurious coach arrived, and they climbed in. He gave a sharp rap on the roof to signal they were ready to leave.

As the lumbering vehicle moved through the crowded streets of Mayfair, they both settled against the blue velvet cushions.

Having inherited his title and lucrative estates at a very young age, Julian had never had to deal with the sort of pressure Michael did. The viscount's wastrel of a father was gambling their earldom into the ground while constantly pressuring Michael to wed an heiress to cover his losses. Julian's own parents had been dead for nearly a decade now, and the title had always seemed like more of a burden than a blessing. It should have been Nathaniel's, not his, and he was reminded of that fact every day.

He met Michael's icy gaze and gave him a sympathetic smile. "Sorry. I can't imagine how hard this must be for you. I'll try to keep my jests to a minimum."

Michael managed a tight smile in return. "I do appreciate the introduction. I'd been at a loss on how to arrange it."

"Think nothing of it," Julian said lightly.

They both became lost in their separate thoughts of the women they'd just left. At least, Julian assumed Michael was thinking about Miss Marks. For his part, he couldn't get Jane out of his mind. When he'd heard that she had let out her house and was sponsoring the American girl this Season, he'd been upset by the news, but now that he'd actually seen her again, he didn't know how he could continue to ignore the situation.

"I've known Jane since we were children. Although never official, there was always an understanding we would wed. I've always been ashamed of myself for not proposing after her father died." As the words left his lips, Julian realized how badly this had been weighing on him, how much he'd needed to talk about it.

"I'd forgotten all about that." Michael offered him a sympathetic glance, seeming glad for the distraction. "It's not your fault the marquess had a gambling problem. No one expected you to marry the girl without a dowry."

"You don't understand. I treated her quite badly, simply walked away and never looked back." Julian winced as he thought of the tears she'd shed that last day that he'd seen her. How many more had she shed because of him? "Perhaps I should arrange an anonymous bequest. I don't want her to have to spend the rest of her life pandering to rich Americans."

Michael braced himself as the coach bounced over a deep rut. "You're not the heartless rake you pretend to be."

"And you're not the staid, joyless paragon you pretend either," Julian retorted. "Come on, old man, admit it. Miss Marks is exactly what you need to make life interesting."

"I admit no such thing," Michael countered, obviously aghast at the very thought.

Julian sighed, turning away to look out the window once again. Now that he truly understood Jane's circumstances, he couldn't ignore them. And now that he'd seen her again, he couldn't pretend that she hadn't been his first—his *only*—love.

She was certainly the only person in his entire life who'd ever truly loved *him.*

WHEN JANE ARRIVED HOME from the theater, she bid Emma goodnight and then hurried up to the sanctuary of her bedroom. She carefully placed the rose Julian had given her in a vase on her dresser then sank down on her bed and stared at it, overwhelmed with riotous emotion.

How dare he!

For seven years, she'd mourned his loss. She'd watched him across crowded ballrooms as he'd flirted and danced with eligible young ladies without a care in the world. As though he'd never told her that he loved her, that she was his best friend, that he couldn't wait to spend the rest of his life with her. He'd made her promises, then broken them recklessly.

Then tonight, out of the blue, he'd decided to impose upon that old friendship. He'd told her that he was glad she'd *returned* to Society, when she'd never left it. Apparently, he hadn't been avoiding her at all those balls and soirees, he just hadn't even noticed that she was there, which was even more insulting! And then, he'd made that stupid silly romantic gesture, gifting her with the rose... and she'd somehow fallen for him all over again. Why did he still have to be so devastatingly handsome? He'd still been a lanky lad in some ways the last time they'd spoken, but now he had the power and grace of a jungle cat. His black hair had gleamed in the candlelight, and she'd wanted to run her fingers through it. His dark eyes still saw too much, holding a deep sadness she wanted to somehow soothe.

I'm such a fool.

She blinked back a rush of tears, furious, confused, and heartsick. How could she still feel something for that notorious womanizer, after everything he'd done to her? She should have refused to make the introductions, given him the cut direct. But she'd needed Emma to meet Lord Sherbourne, so she'd swallowed back the first rush of dismay upon seeing him, only to be taken in by his charm once more.

Now, she had a very bad feeling that Emma and Sherbourne's courtship would entail that she and Julian would be forced to see each other again. How would she bear it?

She loved Emma, but she hated the dire financial straits that had required her to open her home and call upon all her social contacts to launch the beautiful American into the *ton*.

Ever since her father's death, she'd managed to hold on to her house and her small staff by being incredibly frugal and making a series of investments with her meager inheritance. But she'd only been able to make it last for so long, and last year, she'd been forced to look for other ways to support herself. Last Season, she'd rented her house out to one of her cousins, who'd allowed her to stay there as well. But she didn't care for him or his wife, who had been unrelentingly condescending and treated her as though she were an unpaid servant, constantly finding faulting and demanding things be changed.

This spring, Jane had started selling a few of the countless pieces of artwork that graced her home. She'd chosen things she didn't particularly care for anyway, but she feared the day when she'd be living in an empty shell, every beautiful thing her family had spent generations collecting sold to keep her from having to sell the house itself.

Then she'd received a letter from Emma's mother, who'd been told that Jane was a lady of spotless reputation and sterling character. She'd begged Jane to launch Emma into society and offered her a staggering amount of money to do so. Enough to keep her finances healthy for another decade, at least. She'd had no choice but to accept the strange proposal.

Despite her spotless reputation, she knew people were looking down their noses at her for her desperate attempts to save herself. Worse yet, they probably felt *sorry* for her, which was even more deplorable. She couldn't stand the thought of anyone pitying her.

If Emma managed to marry Viscount Sherbourne, Jane would probably make it through this for the most part unscathed, because Emma would take her own place in society, and the *ton* would have to accept her. But if Emma did anything to bring scandal down upon herself, Jane knew she'd be painted with the same brush.

For that reason, it was incredibly important Emma marry Lord Sherbourne. If that meant that Jane had to deal with Julian Tremaine for the next few months, then she was going to have to find a way to endure it. Surely, he'd soon grow tired of trying to pretend that there was still anything between them.

In fact, the more that she thought about it, the less likely it seemed that he'd continue to put himself in close proximity to her. She *had* to accompany Emma on all her outings, but there was no reason that Julian had to accompany Sherbourne.

Feeling slightly better, she started to undress for bed, forcing herself to put all thoughts of Julian out of her head. She refused to entertain the possibility that tonight had changed anything between them. He'd already broken her heart once.

She'd be the worst kind of fool to give him the chance to do it again.

Chapter Two

The next morning, while Jane was dressing for the day, her ladies' maid informed her that Viscount Sherbourne had come to call upon Emma. Jane frowned, wondering why Emma hadn't immediately alerted her. As Emma's companion and chaperone, it was her duty to make sure nothing untoward happened between the courting couple. Giving herself one last look in the mirror, she noted that by piling her hair in a tight chignon and donning a steel-gray morning gown that did not flatter her in the least, she'd managed to age herself dramatically.

The emotional upheaval of her interaction with Basingstoke last night had shown her that she could no longer pretend that she had any prospects whatsoever. She was twenty-five years old, and no knight in shining armor was coming to save her. She'd never be a wife or mother. The sooner she came to terms with her spinster status, the better.

Her tumbling thoughts came to an abrupt halt when she entered the drawing room and caught sight of Emma. Her charge reclined upon a sofa wearing nothing but a purple satin robe, her lovely dark hair streaming around her slim shoulders. Jane was so stunned that for a moment she couldn't even speak. This was bad. So very bad. She saw her reputation—the only thing she really had left— going down in flames along with Emma's. What had the girl been thinking? Had she lost her mind?

"Good God, Emma," she finally managed. "Please tell me you didn't receive Viscount Sherbourne in your dressing gown. Whatever must he think of you?"

Emma grinned, seeming very pleased with herself. "He thinks I'm a little better than a whore. But he wants to marry me anyway."

The lecture on propriety died on Jane's lips. "Sherbourne proposed?" Relief poured through her, and she raced across the room to give her young friend an exuberant hug. "Oh, Emma. How wonderful. He's exactly what you've been looking for."

Despite Emma's beauty and obscenely large dowry, finding her quality suitors had proved quite the challenge. Her brash, bubbly personality had proved too much for most titled gentlemen, who wanted meek and biddable wives.

"Yes. He's absolutely perfect." Despite her brazen behavior, Emma seemed brittle in Jane's embrace, obviously not as confident about the entire matter as she wanted Jane to think. "Sherbourne needs my dowry desperately." Emma ducked out of Jane's embrace. "He didn't even try to deny it."

Jane frowned. "Well, we knew that, of course. But I expected him to propose more gracefully. He should have made more of an effort to court you." Sherbourne's actions had been just as disgraceful as Emma's. What sort of gentleman arrived to propose at such an unreasonably early hour the day after they'd been introduced?

"He considers his proposal a business arrangement." Emma bit her lip, finally letting her doubts show. She'd insisted that all she cared about was getting a title, and marrying Sherbourne would eventually make her a countess, but she had to want more from her life than that.

"Surely, romance will come in time," Jane tried to reassure her. "I sensed a strong attraction between the two of you."

"He's the most beautiful man I've ever met." Emma shrugged, a sudden smile curving her lips. "Perhaps I will marry your haughty young viscount," she told Jane conspiratorially. "But I'm not going to give him an answer right away. In fact, I have every intention of making him wonder."

Jane forced a laugh, wishing she had even an ounce of Emma's self-confidence. One did not make a man like Viscount Sherbourne wait! But even though Jane knew the rules and etiquette of polite society, she was wise enough to admit that she knew nothing of how to seduce a man, a knowledge Emma seemed to have been born with.

"Well, I'm sure you and Sherbourne will be able to work things out." Jane fingered the high neckline of her unflattering gown, a surge of sadness overwhelming her. She wanted the best for Emma, but she had to admit that she'd enjoyed having the young woman around. She supposed she could take on another American heiress after Emma left, but then that girl would leave her, too.

All she'd ever wanted was for someone to love her enough to stay.

JULIAN WAS SURPRISED when his butler escorted Sherbourne into his study the next afternoon. Sherbourne had never arrived unannounced before As his old friend took a seat on the other side of Julian's desk, he looked both terrified and excited.

"I did it," Sherbourne stated without preamble.

"Did what?" Julian asked blankly, pushing aside the account books he'd been working on to give his friend his full attention.

"I proposed to Miss Marks," Sherbourne replied with a note of exasperation, as though Julian should have known.

"Miss Marks?" Julian blinked, utterly taken aback. He'd known Sherbourne since they were lads and had never once known the man to do anything so rash. "You mean the girl you just met yesterday?"

"I decided there was no reason to drag the matter out. If she won't have me, I'll have to find someone else." Sherbourne shrugged uncomfortably. "The creditors are nipping at my heels. I don't have much time before my father completely ruins us."

Julian knew how hard it was for his friend to admit such a thing. Sherbourne was nothing if not prideful. "I had no idea things had gotten this bad. Perhaps I could loan you enough to tide you over?"

Sherbourne gave him a quelling look. "I appreciate the offer, but I couldn't possibly take your charity."

"Well, think it over," Julian insisted. "It seems a far better plan than marrying a girl you don't know the first thing about."

Scrubbing a hand across his wan face, Sherbourne managed an uneasy chuckle. "Can I tell you something in the strictest confidence?"

Julian leaned forward, intrigued. Though he considered Michael one of his closest friends, they weren't in the habit of sharing secrets. "Of course. Consider me a vault."

Sherbourne shook his head. "When I arrived, she kept me waiting for an eternity, then came down to greet me wearing nothing but a purple satin dressing gown." He leaned back in his chair. "She is exquisite. I was utterly flummoxed. Made an utter ass of myself. She agreed to think about it but didn't give me an answer. I feel I've ruined everything."

The look of abject misery on Sherbourne's face was the only thing that kept Julian from laughing outright. He couldn't imagine his straitlaced friend confronted by such outlandish behavior. "Do you think she was having you on? Trying to see how you'd react?"

"I think that's exactly what she was doing," Sherbourne replied in a disgruntled tone. "I just didn't think I'd be so... affected by her. She's so lovely, so exciting. She terrifies me, if I'm being perfectly honest."

This time, Julian couldn't hold back his laughter. He felt for his friend, he truly did. But all he could think about was that this would give him another chance with Jane. He had a lot to make up for, and he knew the odds of her forgiving him were not in his favor. But he was no longer the stupid, selfish boy he'd once been, and he was determined to at least try. If nothing else, he wanted to find a way to help her financially, though he sensed that would be a battle as well, given her prideful independent streak.

OVER THE NEXT WEEK, Emma ran Viscount Sherbourne a merry chase, but at last, she agreed to his proposal. The morning after, she enlisted Jane's help in penning a missive to her father. In it, she extolled Michael's virtues and lineage, then pleaded with Blackjack Marks, the famous American railroad tycoon, to travel to London as quickly as possible.

"Don't look so worried," Jane said, once they'd sent a footman to post the letter. "Sherbourne is one of the best catches in England. Your father will be thrilled."

"It's not my father I'm worried about." Emma shrugged. "What if I'm making a terrible mistake? Michael can be such a terrible snob."

"You didn't seem to mind when the two of you disappeared from the ball last night. You were practically glowing when you returned." Jane had struggled mightily with her decision to let Emma sneak away with Sherbourne. She'd sensed that they needed a moment of privacy, but it had been a terrible risk. She shuddered to think what would have happened if anyone had caught them.

"Honestly, Jane. Sometimes you take your role as chaperone just a little too far." Emma's words held no real heat. The two women had built a solid friendship despite their differences. Jane liked to think they complemented each other.

"You don't need a chaperone, Emma," Jane teased. "You need a keeper."

Emma laughed and slanted an arch look at Jane. "Lord Basingstoke will be at dinner tonight. Perhaps I'll be the one who will need to chaperone you."

Earlier, a beautifully handwritten invitation had arrived, asking Emma and Jane to a celebratory dinner at Michael's father's house. When she'd found out Julian was going to be there, she'd wanted mightily to decline, but she couldn't. Wherever Emma went, she must go also.

Jane felt her face heat with embarrassment. "Lord Basingstoke meant nothing by his little display at the theater. He's always been a bit of a showoff."

"Lord Basingstoke?" Emma raised a brow. "Just a few nights ago, he was Julian."

Jane sighed and met Emma's knowing gaze. "A mere slip of the tongue. We knew each other as children and his immature antics made me regress."

"Oh, I see." Emma fought a smile.

Jane sank into the chair across from her and poured the tea from the breakfast tray, her practiced movements far less graceful than usual. "Are you nervous about dining with Lord Warren?"

"Yes, I am a little nervous," Emma admitted, allowing Jane to change the subject. "He's quite intimidating. I'm not sure how he'll react to the thought of an American daughter-in-law."

"He'll hate it," Jane replied. "But don't take it personally. He'd manage to find fault with anybody Sherbourne chose." She'd known the Blakes since she was a child, and the earl had always made her uncomfortable. He'd been cruel and abusive to Michael's younger brother, Dylan, and he'd pressured Michael to become the perfect heir until he'd nearly snapped.

"Well, I'll just have to do my best to charm him, won't I?" Emma gave Jane a brief smile. "Help me find something to wear, Jane. Something very conservative."

Jane took a quick mental inventory of Emma's flamboyant wardrobe and then shook her head. "I don't think you own anything conservative enough for dinner with the Earl of Warren. You'll have to borrow something of mine."

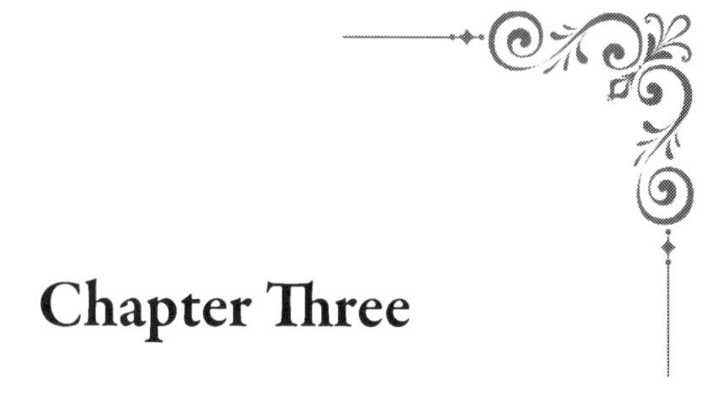

Chapter Three

When Sherbourne sent round a note asking Julian to join him, Miss Marks, Jane, and his father, the formidable Earl of Warren, for dinner to celebrate his engagement, Julian hastily agreed. Michael had a terrible relationship with his father, and Julian knew his friend wanted him to be there for moral support.

He arrived before the women, and Sherbourne's look of relief was palpable. "Thanks for coming," his friend told him, pulling him into a swift embrace that was completely unlike him.

Realizing that Sherbourne was truly nervous about the coming evening, Julian patted him comfortingly on the back before stepping away. "It will be all right."

Michael laughed bitterly and turned to pour them both a drink. "My father is furious that I've gone ahead with this. He acts as though he's given me any choice. As though there were a dozen other heiresses beating down my door."

Julian accepted the drink and lifted it toward his friend in a sympathetic salute. "You did the right thing in refusing to marry Lady Natalia. She loves Dylan, and both of you would have been miserable if you'd made her give him up. You'll be much happier with Miss Marks." The woman the earl had chosen for Michael—Lady Natalia Sinclair, the daughter of a duke and also a great heiress—had run off a few weeks ago with Michael's younger brother, Dylan, who was estranged from the family and wouldn't contribute a farthing to their cause.

"Happy?" Sherbourne scoffed as if he'd never heard of such a thing. "I don't know if I'll ever be happy as long as my father lives."

Before Julian could respond, the butler announced the women. Julian didn't even hear the man's words because the moment he caught sight of Jane, his heart squeezed in his chest. Her honey-blond hair was piled atop her head in a loose chignon, and her teal gown hugged her lush curves like a second skin, leaving little to the imagination. The creamy swells of her breasts took his breath away, and he forced himself to move his gaze to her warm blue eyes.

She seemed to be just as stricken as he, a faint flush on her lovely face as she stared at him with a longing she couldn't hide. Memories of the past, of the kisses and confidences they'd shared and the love and support she'd given him during the hardest part of his life nearly overwhelmed him. *What have I done? How could I have been so stupid?*

He moved toward her, as though pulled by a thread, hoping she could see the sincerity in his eyes as he bent over her hand. "Good evening, Lady Jane. You're looking lovely tonight."

Her face flamed even brighter. "Thank you, Lord Basingstoke. You're looking very well yourself."

For the next ten or fifteen minutes, the four of them engaged in polite small talk, but although Julian couldn't take his eyes off Jane, he gradually became aware of Michael's growing unease.

"I don't know what could be keeping my father," Michael finally said, snapping his pocket watch closed. "I'll go see what's keeping him."

The moment Michael left the room, Emma's face fell. "The earl is refusing to come to dinner, isn't he? He objects to our marriage so thoroughly he can't even pretend to be polite."

"I'm sure that's not the case," Julian tried to assure her but knowing the old bastard as he did, he very much feared her words to be true.

Jane tried to distract her protégé with a tidbit of gossip as Julian paced the room, casting occasional covert looks at Jane while trying to think of a way to get her alone this evening. Though she was Emma's chaperone, surely it would be all right for her to leave the engaged couple alone for a few minutes? He glanced at the clock with a frown. Given Emma's rising agitation, he began to wonder if she'd call the whole thing off.

Nearly half an hour passed before Michael finally returned with his obviously disgruntled father in tow. Dinner was unbearable. Even though Julian had been warned, he couldn't believe the way Warren behaved. The earl was terribly rude to Emma, then stormed out halfway through the meal, claiming he had another engagement.

Silence reigned in the dining room for several moments after the earl took his leave, and Jane exchanged a shocked look with Julian, both of them stunned by the way Michael's father had treated his future daughter-in-law.

Recovering herself, Miss Marks drained her glass of wine and got to her feet. "I just remembered that I also have another pressing engagement." Her words were carefully precise, but the pain in her voice gave her away. "Shall we go, Jane?"

Jane gave an uncertain nod.

Michael cast a pleading glance in Julian's direction, obviously hoping he would take pity on him. "Julian, would you escort Lady Jane down to the conservatory and show her the orchids? I'd like a few moments alone with Miss Marks."

Julian frowned even though he wanted nothing more than to escape to the conservatory with Jane. Miss Marks had done well under the earl's insults, holding her own and refusing to cower as he'd wanted, but she looked on the verge of tears. He met her dark gaze, finding himself on her side in this matter. If she wanted to leave, he wasn't going to impede her. "Is that all right with you, Miss Marks? I can call for your coachman, if you prefer."

Michael threw Julian a glare, then got to his feet and came to stand behind his fiancée, touching her shoulder tentatively. "Please. I need to talk to you."

Miss Marks cleared her throat then nodded jerkily. "As a matter of fact, there are some things I want to say to you, too."

Julian shook his head. Poor Michael. Miss Marks was no wilting flower and seemed rightfully upset that Michael hadn't stood up to his father on her behalf. She'd probably give him an earful once they were alone. Michael would be lucky if she let the engagement stand.

He turned his gaze on Jane, wondering if he'd fare any better than Michael. Jane had years' worth of anger to share with him, he was sure. But ever since she'd reentered his life the other day, she'd been haunting his thoughts. He had to at least try to mend things between them.

He stood and went to her side, taking her hand and drawing her to her feet. Her scent, a lovely combination of lavender and vanilla, filled his senses. "Shall we?" he asked softly.

"We'll be back shortly," Jane promised, a worried look on her face as he steered her toward the door.

JANE ENDURED THE SLIGHT pressure of Julian's hand on her waist until they were safely away from the dining room. Then she shook him off, desperate to hide the fact that his slightest touch still had the power to turn her into a lovesick fool.

She hated herself for her weakness. This man had destroyed her. How was it possible to still want him so badly? All during the interminable dinner, she'd found her gaze drawn to him repeatedly, much to her chagrin. He'd caught her staring at him more than once, but she'd tried to play it off, tried to pretend that he wasn't the most handsome man she'd ever seen.

Julian paused, staring down at her with those moody dark eyes that always saw too much. "Do you hate me, Jane?"

Stunned by his blunt question, she stepped back, inadvertently trapping herself between the wall and Julian's big lean body. "You give yourself far too much credit, Julian. I haven't even thought about you in years."

He moved in and braced his hands on either side of her head, a faint smile curving his lips. "Liar."

His scent overwhelmed her, the intoxicating mix of leather and man that dredged up memories best left forgotten. Taking a deep breath, she placed her hands on the muscular wall of his chest and tried to shove him away. "Surely, you have better things to do than toy with the emotions of a spinster."

He refused to budge, and she knew she'd made a terrible tactical error. The warm, tantalizing swell of his chest teased her fingers. The desire to touch him overwhelmed her.

"Oh, Jane," he murmured. "You're far too lovely to be a spinster. I can't believe that you are. I thought you'd married someone else ages ago."

"If you cared at all, you would have kept track of me." She shook her head. "You're the one who hasn't given *me* a second thought."

"I'm thinking of you now. Ever since I saw you the other night at the theater, I've been remembering how it used to be between us... How you used to kiss me so sweetly..." He lowered his head and pressed his lips to her forehead, a tender caress that made her ache for what could have been.

She closed her eyes against him and prayed for strength. "I was a fool, Julian. I believed you when you said you loved me."

"Maybe I did love you." His voice was low and rough, his mouth mere inches from her ear. "God knows I've never felt that way about anyone else."

"You didn't love me." At last, her disappointment managed to eclipse the need to be in his arms again. She ducked beneath his arm and glared at him from a few feet away. "You ran away from me when I needed you most."

Julian remained where he was, one arm braced against the wall, the other clenched at his side. "I'm sorry. I was criminally stupid. Can you ever forgive me?"

"No." Jane resisted the urge to smooth the dark silky hair from his forehead. "It's too late for that, Julian. Years too late."

He didn't protest when she spun on her heels and took her leave, going to wait for Emma in the foyer, her hands trembling as she put on her wrap. Stupid tears stung her eyes, and she was forced to admit that she'd hoped that he would come after her, that he'd act as though he really meant his apology. But he was obviously just trying to be polite, trying to make things easier, since they were going to see so much of each other over the coming months.

As she squared her shoulders and forced the tears away, she knew she'd do practically anything for the chance to cheat time. If only she could go back to that summer when she'd been seventeen and Julian Tremaine had been the center of her world...

She could still remember the first time he'd kissed her, the way they'd held each other and whispered secrets. They'd created their own little world at the hunting cottage on her father's land, and she'd truly thought it would last forever. Those had undoubtedly been the best days of her life.

But his betrayal had wounded her deeply, so much so that she'd turned down the few prospective suitors she'd had in the years since. She'd given up on all thoughts of marrying or having a family of her own, all because she couldn't risk being hurt that deeply again.

She had to keep reminding herself of that and ignore his sweet words and insincere apologies.

Chapter Four

"I need to talk to you," Jane told Emma later that evening, perching on the edge of a small sofa when they arrived back at her townhouse. "It's about Julian."

She couldn't keep her feelings to herself any longer. For too long, she'd held her anger for Julian deep inside her, telling no one what had happened all those years ago. In truth, she'd never really allowed herself to get close to *anyone* since Julian had hurt her so deeply. Still, despite the financial aspect of their relationship, she and Emma had become good friends, and she desperately needed a friend now. She needed someone to tell her that she'd been right to walk away from him tonight.

Emma sank into the chair across from Jane, her troubled dark eyes brightening a bit. She'd been very quiet on the ride home, and Jane knew she was grappling with doubts of her own. The earl had treated her deplorably, and Michael had not defended her as he should have. "Tell me everything. I'm absolutely dying to know."

"I love him," Jane admitted, the words spilling out of her far more quickly than she'd intended. "I've loved him since I was a child."

"Oh, Jane," Emma whispered sadly, immediately understanding the futility of her sentiments.

Jane buried her face in her hands, unable to look her friend in the eyes. "His country estate bordered my father's. He was eight the first time I met him. I'm sure you can imagine how he dazzled my six-year-old country heart. He went away to school, so I didn't see him for many years, but he returned when he inherited the title. There was such an air of tragedy about him. He'd lost nearly all his family in a series of unfortunate accidents, and I wanted to comfort him."

Emma moved to sit beside her and placed a consoling arm around her shoulders. "Well, you must have succeeded. I certainly wouldn't describe him as tragic now."

Jane lifted her head, tears springing to her eyes. "Oh, but he *is* tragic. He's just grown so much better at hiding it." She dropped her gaze and twisted her hands in her lap. "I'm afraid I let him take dreadful liberties, Emma. My only defense is that I loved him so much. I couldn't imagine his feelings were not as strong as mine."

"What happened?" Emma asked.

Jane drew a deep shuddering breath. "My father died, and Julian didn't seem to know how to be there for me the way I'd always been there for him. He distanced himself, went to London, and before long, I started hearing rumors that he'd been courting other women."

"Oh, Jane. I'm so sorry."

Jane shrugged. "I'm embarrassed to admit how long I waited for him to come back. Months. Years, perhaps. I rejected other suitable prospects, until eventually, I found myself with no prospects at all. And now, all these years later, after I was so certain I'd finally gotten over him, here he is, once again in my life. I don't know what he's playing at or why he's pretending a renewed interest in me. Perhaps he just finds it amusing to tie my heart in knots."

"What happened tonight?" Emma asked. "Did he kiss you?"

"I think he would have," Jane admitted. "I think he wanted to."

"But you ran away," Emma guessed, obviously remembering that Jane had been standing alone in the foyer when they'd left.

"Of course, I ran away. If I'd stayed, I might have forgiven him."

"Would that really be such a bad thing? It's been a long time. Perhaps he's changed."

"Nothing's changed," Jane insisted. "He's incapable of loving anyone."

JULIAN WENT DIRECTLY to his club after leaving the Earl of Warren's townhouse, hoping to drown his sorrows in the bottom of a bottle. He settled at a corner table with a glass of brandy, staring into the fireplace as he contemplated all the ways the night had gone horribly wrong.

What had he expected? That Jane would willingly fall back into his arms again after all this time?

Perhaps he had. Perhaps he'd been dealing with courtesans and fallen women for so long that he'd forgotten how to actually woo a good woman.

Jane *was* a good woman. The very best. He didn't deserve her, wasn't even sure he *wanted* her, so what the hell was he doing? It wasn't as though he could take her as his mistress.

He'd never suggest such a thing or dishonor her in such a way. No, despite her unwarranted spinster status, Jane was still very marriageable. If anything, she was even lovelier now than when she'd been eighteen.

A week ago, he'd been completely satisfied with his bachelor status. He'd had no plans of ever marrying and would have been glad to go to his grave without ever having secured his line. But now...

Now he couldn't stop remembering his first taste of love, how good Jane had been to him during the most trying time of his life.

He'd been just fourteen when his older brother and younger sister had died in a tragic accident. A year later, his mother had wasted away from grief and joined them. Three years later, his father had drunk himself to death, leaving Julian an earl at the age of eighteen. When he'd left school and arrived at his family's country estate to assume his duties, it had been Jane who'd helped him through it.

They'd met in the woods that joined her father's estate with his. With her, he'd finally been able to talk about his pain and anger. She'd been the one to help him understand that he needed to quit blaming his younger brother Ethan for what had happened to their siblings. She'd made him understand that his parents had been so lost in their own grief that they'd stopped being parents, but that it wasn't his fault and he shouldn't hate them.

She'd been his best friend, his confidante, and the only safe place in his life. There had been stolen kisses and heavy petting, but she'd never let him go any further, and he hadn't pressed her, because he'd truly had every intention of marrying her.

Then her father had died, and their roles had reversed.

He glanced down at his glass and was surprised to find it empty. Grimacing, he gestured for another.

A few moments after the waiter brought him his second drink, an acquaintance of his slid into the chair opposite him. Christian Hunter, Viscount Harding, had been a schoolmate of Julian's younger brother, Ethan. The two had been very close, but he didn't know the man well at all himself. Still, he welcomed the interruption of his maudlin thoughts.

"Basingstoke," Harding murmured. "May I have a moment of your time?"

Julian raised a sardonic brow. "Seems you already have it."

Harding had the good grace to flush a bit. "Sorry. You seem as though you're enjoying your solitude tonight, but I wanted to ask something of you, and I'm not certain when I'll next have a chance to talk to you alone."

Julian frowned. "This sounds serious." He couldn't imagine what the man wanted from him.

"It's about Ethan," Harding said, lowering his gaze to the table. "I need him to come back to England."

The mere mention of his younger brother tied Julian's heart in knots, as it always did. He missed him dreadfully, longed to set things right between them, but he didn't have the faintest clue where to start.

"I'm afraid you've come to the wrong person," he said sharply. "Surely, you know that Ethan hates me. I'm the last person who could convince him to do anything."

It had been Ethan's idea to go ice skating on the pond behind the castle, even though their father had strictly forbidden them from doing so until he had a chance to test the ice. However, their father had been in London, and they hadn't known when he'd return. Ethan had convinced his twin, Elizabeth, to join him. When she'd fallen through the ice, their older brother, Nathaniel, had tried to save her, only to fall through himself. Ethan had run for help, but by the time he'd come back with a rope and some of the groomsmen, it had been too late. Nathaniel and Elizabeth were already gone.

Their father had blamed Ethan, beaten him senseless, then sent him away to school. Julian had parroted his father's hateful words, lost in his own grief and despair. He'd realized fairly soon after that he'd been wrong, that it had simply been a horrible accident, and that Ethan wasn't to blame. Hell, he'd gone out on the ice himself just the day before. It could just as easily been him that Nathaniel had died saving. But by then, the rift had already been made, and he'd never known how to breach it.

Was he forever doomed to drive away those he loved most?

Harding sighed. "He stays in South America because he believes you hate him. I just thought that perhaps it was time the two of you talked. That perhaps if you asked him, if you made sure he knew that you no longer blamed him for the past, that he might come home."

Julian frowned. "Why do you need him to come home?"

"He's my best friend, and I miss him," Harding said simply. His voice broke and he looked away. "I'm very sick, and I want to see him again while there's still time."

For the first time, Julian noticed how pale and thin Harding had become. He would have assumed he'd simply been spending too much time drinking and partaking in the seedy underside of Society if the man hadn't confessed his illness. Sudden sympathy for the man flooded him.

Perhaps fate had a hand in this. Maybe it was time for him to mend his fences with Jane *and* Ethan. Harding's illness reminded him that life was fleeting. If he didn't apologize now, when would he? His time wasn't infinite.

"What did you have in mind?" he asked Harding.

LATER THAT EVENING, lying alone in his huge bed, Julian found himself taking a long hard look at his past. He forced himself to confront his actions regarding Ethan and Jane, and he found himself ashamed to the depths of his soul.

He'd loved Jane, truly loved her. She'd once been the most important person in his entire world. He'd been so damaged and broken, but she'd somehow managed to put him back together again, piece by careful piece, with her kindness and purity of spirit.

She'd given her love unconditionally, never asking for anything in return. How could he have walked away from that?

Every moment he'd spent in her company during the last week had only served to crack his heart open a little more, until the love he'd once had for her had returned and even multiplied. It had all made him realize how tired he was of the life he'd been living. He hadn't lied when he'd told Michael he only intended to marry for love. He knew now that all this time he'd been searching for what he'd found with Jane when he was young.

How foolish he'd been to think that he'd find that sort of connection and respect again.

The big question, now that he'd found that feeling again, was what he planned to do about it.

He punched his pillow and turned on his side, gazing into the dying flames of the fire. *I want to marry her. I never should have let her down, and if she'll have me, I'd be happy to spend the rest of my life making it up to her.*

Once the thought entered his mind, it wouldn't leave. He'd always been meant to be Jane's husband. She suited him so perfectly, the perfect combination of innocence and sensuality, a friend he could count on, no matter what.

Now all he had to do was convince her that she could count on him as well.

It wouldn't be easy, given the terrible mistakes he'd made in the past, but he'd changed. He was ready now, and somehow, he had to make her see that.

A small smile curved his lips as he imagined how he might go about seducing his beautiful spinster to come around to his way of thinking.

Chapter Five

Jane couldn't believe she'd let Emma talk her into accompanying her to Julian's house a week after the disastrous dinner party. She should have known it was merely an excuse for her friend to be alone with Michael. Things were very unsettled between them, as Emma had wanted to be married in New York and Michael had been forced to admit that his financial situation was so dire that he had no time left for such things. He'd insisted they be married immediately or not at all.

Jane also should have known Julian was under orders to spirit her away so the engaged couple could have a few moments to themselves to talk about all the obstacles that stood between them. While an obvious physical attraction seethed between Michael and Emma, Jane wasn't at all certain the two of them would be happy together. They simply seemed far too different.

The fact that Jane had willingly gone with Julian—and hadn't uttered a word of protest when he suggested they view the portrait gallery—only proved she was the most weak-willed woman who'd ever lived. She'd shirked her duties as Emma's chaperone in order to spend a few more moments alone with the man who'd broken her heart beyond repair.

"I don't know what you hoped to accomplish by bringing me up here," she told Julian, once they entered the long echoing room.

Julian only laughed. "Why, Lady Jane. You give yourself far too much credit. I haven't given you a second thought in years."

She blushed, hating the ease with which he turned her own words against her, making them sound like the lie that they were. Of course, in his case, they were probably true. She certainly harbored no illusions that he'd given much thought to her at all over the last seven years.

"We really shouldn't leave Emma and Michael alone together. I'm supposed to be acting as her chaperone."

Julian came up behind her and put his big hands on her shoulders. The heat of his touch stole her breath away. "What harm can it do if they want to explore the passionate feelings they have for one another?" he murmured, his voice very near her ear. "They'll be married in less than a week."

He was right, of course, but she hated that she had nothing left to argue with him about. She stared blindly at a portrait of Julian's family, commissioned scant months before the tragedy that had torn them apart forever, and tried to ignore the overwhelming presence of the flesh and blood man behind her.

He flexed his hands, tenderly massaging her shoulders, and she fought the urge to crumple into a puddle at his feet. Realizing how dangerous even this casual touch could be, she stepped away, trying to leave a comfortable distance between them.

"All right," he told her. "I understand. You don't want to renew our friendship. And you're right. You have every reason to view me with suspicion. But before we part ways, I must know what will happen to you once Miss Marks is wed."

Frowning, she took another step away from him. "I don't know what you mean."

"Just this. You don't have to take in another American to keep a roof over your head." He sighed and raked one hand through his dark hair. "Let me help you, Jane."

She stared at him, aghast and embarrassed. "I don't need your help."

He closed the distance between them, as though he knew she couldn't think clearly while he was this close. "Stubborn," he muttered. "You always have been."

Relieved that he seemed to have accepted her refusal, she forced herself to relax. "I've struggled to make ends meet for years now, and you never seemed to care. Why the sudden interest?"

Julian stared at her. Again, she found herself drowning in the depths of his midnight eyes. "I tried to forget you. Hell, perhaps I even succeeded for a while. But you're the only woman I've ever known who truly knew me, and I miss that. I miss you."

Jane squared her shoulders, determined to resist him. "That was a long time ago. You're a stranger to me now."

"Then get to know me again," he pleaded, his heart in his eyes. "Let me court you, Jane."

Court me?

For a moment, the whole world seemed to shift, to expand. *Dear God.* This was what she'd always wanted. To marry Julian and bear his children. To make a home for him and soothe away his demons. "You can't be serious."

"Oh, I am," he assured her. "What must I do to prove it to you?"

"I don't know," she whispered, turning away. Once more, her gaze fell on the portrait of Julian's family. She seized upon it, needing to change the subject. "Do you ever speak to Ethan?"

"No. He left the country the moment he graduated from Cambridge. He was chasing after orchids in the jungles of South America, last I heard."

The hint of wistfulness in his voice surprised her. He blamed his younger brother for the accident that had taken the lives of his older brother and little sister, or at least he once had.

She turned to look at him, trying to see past the hooded wariness in his dark eyes. "Do you still hate him for what happened?"

Julian sighed. "Of course not. He was just a child when Elizabeth and Nathaniel died. And he wasn't the only one who went skating despite Father's warnings."

"Oh, Julian," she whispered. "You should write him a letter. Let him know. I'm sure he'd like to mend the rift between you."

"Maybe you're right. In fact, a friend of his asked me to do exactly that just a few days ago. But I don't know what to say after all these years." Julian closed his eyes, and the stark sadness on his chiseled features made her regret raising the topic. She'd never meant to hurt him.

"You'll find the words. Just do it soon, or you'll regret it forever." As she spoke, she stepped into his arms. She couldn't help herself.

Julian inhaled sharply and pulled her against him, burying his face in her hair. "You realize you're one of the only people

I know who even remembers I have a brother?" He cupped her face and lifted her head, staring at her with such hungry intensity it took her breath away. "You know me better than anyone else in the world. How can you pretend otherwise?"

Confused, terrified of her own conflicting emotions, she stepped out of his grasp. "We *were* friends, Julian. But that was a long time ago. And I'm sorry, but I can't trust you. I can't let you hurt me again."

Desperate to escape—before she listened to her heart and agreed to this foolishness—she hurried down the hall toward the cozy little sitting room where they'd left Emma and Michael.

"Jane. Don't go. There's so much more I want to say to you..." Julian's swift steps echoed behind her.

She increased her pace, afraid to stop, afraid to spend even one more moment alone with him. When she finally reached the sitting room, she threw the door open without knocking.

She realized her mistake a second too late.

Emma and Michael lay tangled together on the sofa, engaged in an act of startling intimacy. Michael's mouth was on Emma's bare breast, and his hand was buried beneath her skirt. Emma's eyes were closed, a look of pure bliss on her face.

Jane drew in a startled breath but couldn't force herself to look away. She'd never seen anything so shocking. Yet the intimately entwined couple had a strange beauty she found all too compelling.

Longing knifed through her. The innocent passion she'd shared with Julian a decade ago had never led to this. Never... except in her lonely, aching dreams. How many times had she fantasized about their passion, wishing she'd let Julian take her innocence, since now it seemed no one ever would?

Julian came to an abrupt halt at her side. Heat suffused her face. She turned to leave, trying to push him out of the room before her.

He tore his gaze away from their friends and gave her a questioning glance. A choked laugh escaped him when he saw the look on her face.

She elbowed him in the stomach, cutting off the sound. But it was too late.

Michael lifted his head, and the mortification in his eyes eclipsed her own embarrassment. "Oh, God," Michael moaned. He scrambled to shield Emma from view.

"I'm sorry," Jane whispered, backing away. "I'm so sorry."

Julian cleared his throat, and she knew he was doing his best to hold back even more laughter. "We'll just wait out here until you're through."

Shutting the door firmly behind him, he shook his head and leaned against the wall, his dark eyes bright with amusement. "What were you thinking, Jane? You expected to find them having tea and discussing China patterns?"

"I don't know." She pressed her hands against her hot cheeks, humiliated. "I will never be able to look Emma in the eyes again."

"Why not?" Julian shoved off the wall and pulled her unwillingly into his embrace. "It's only passion. Don't you remember what it was like to feel passion?"

She remembered far too well. And trapped as she was, utterly surrounded by his lean strength, all she could think about was the rapturous look on Emma's face.

Oh, how she envied her friend for having the courage to risk her heart.

But as she stared up into Julian's burning dark eyes, she knew she couldn't do this. She didn't have Emma's courage, or perhaps she just couldn't imagine ever trusting him again.

"I need some more time," she whispered, slipping out of his embrace. "If you're really serious about courting me, you're going to have to prove you've changed." She couldn't even believe she was giving him that much, but what she'd just seen had made her realize how desperately lonely she was, how the only time she'd been truly happy was when she was with the man next to her.

He raked his hands through his dark hair in frustration. "What do you want from me? How can I prove such a thing?"

She shook her head, tears stinging her eyes. "I don't know, Julian. I only know I'm not ready to fall into your arms again just yet."

"WELL." AFTER THEY'D seen the girls off, Julian hid a smile and poured himself and Michael both a stiff drink. "It seems as though your courtship with Miss Marks is proceeding smashingly well."

Michael accepted the drink, though he shot Julian a fulminating glare over the rim as he drained it. "A gentleman would let the matter rest," he snapped. "He certainly wouldn't be sniffing around for more details."

"Lucky for you, I'm not a gentleman then, isn't it?" Julian leaned forward and refilled Michael's glass, raising an eyebrow at the speed with which he'd downed it. "Because I can't let this rest until I'm certain you'll stop feeling guilty over what happened. Hell, I'm happy to see you're human. She's good for you. You know that, don't you?"

Michael shook his head. "I was starting to think so, but now I'm not so sure. Christ, I can't think of anything except bedding her."

Julian laughed.

"It's not funny. I completely lost control tonight. What if it had been someone other than you and Jane to open that door?"

"Well, it wasn't, so stop berating yourself. Emma obviously isn't sorry about what happened, so why should you be?"

"That's another thing," Michael admitted. "She's the most passionate woman I've ever known. I fear if she starts straying outside our marriage, I won't be able to bear it."

"You love her," Julian observed soberly.

Michael closed his eyes and scrubbed his hand over his face in dismay. "I certainly didn't feel this insane protectiveness over Natalia."

Julian sighed. "Why are you so certain Emma will stray?"

"They all stray," Michael muttered. "My mother—" He broke off and shook his head. "She was repeatedly unfaithful to my father. In fact, I think that's why he's so bitter, so unable to love anyone. Even his own children."

Julian frowned and tossed back the contents of his glass. "I'm sure the earl was an insufferable bastard long before he met your mother. And you mustn't judge her too harshly. You haven't the slightest idea what drove her to take a lover, if she really did. Besides, your parents have absolutely nothing to do with your future bride."

Michael held out his glass for yet another refill. "I don't know how everything got so complicated."

"Such is life." Julian shrugged philosophically. "You should be in my shoes, my friend. At least you and Emma are starting with a clean slate. I have years of past sins to atone for where Jane is concerned."

Michael frowned. "You can't mean to make her your mistress. She's an innocent. A lady."

Julian glared at him. "Is it so inconceivable that my intentions for Lady Jane might be honorable?"

"Yes," Michael answered, his surprise making him uncharacteristically tactless. "You told me just the other day you never intended to marry."

"I said I never intended to marry someone I didn't love." Julian shook his head and strode across the room, turning his back on Michael as he stared out the window. "I've never loved anyone the way I loved Jane. I admit it scared the hell out of me." He met Michael's gaze over his shoulder. "So, I walked away. I lost everything because I didn't have the courage to trust her."

Michael looked away, unable to meet his gaze.

Julian sighed. "Don't let your past ruin your future," he admonished. "That's hard-won wisdom, so don't take it lightly." Then, he turned and strode from the room, leaving Michael alone to ponder his words.

As he headed home, he couldn't stop remembering the pain in Jane's voice when she'd told him how he'd hurt her.

Frustrated, he slammed his hand against the side of his carriage, relishing the sharp pain. He'd laid his heart bare tonight, once again thinking that it would be enough. But it wasn't. He'd hurt her too badly.

And she'd brought up Ethan.... It seemed too much of a coincidence that both she and Harding had urged him to mend things with his brother.

His mistakes were catching up to him. He only hoped he had the strength to prove his love to those who mattered most.

Chapter Six

Julian rode up to Sherbourne Hall two days before Michael and Emma's wedding. He was pleased to find Michael's brother, Dylan, and his new wife, Natalia, had already arrived. He spent a few minutes chatting with his old friend, who seemed uncommonly distracted, but before he could ask Dylan what was wrong, Emma's retinue came up the long drive, and the moment was lost.

He watched from the front steps at Michael went out to greet his future bride, noticing that things still seemed tense between them. He hoped that they managed to find some happiness together, but this certainly wasn't an auspicious beginning. Emma had been forced to lower her expectations time and again, giving up everything she'd wanted her wedding to be and accepting this rushed affair simply so Michael could get his hands on her dowry as soon as possible. Julian knew his friend was under immense stress and strain, but he couldn't help but feel that he ought to be trying a little harder to woo his lovely fiancée.

Jane and Emma's father, Black Jack Marks, the American industrialist, followed the couple into the castle, and everyone chatted for a while before the new arrivals all went to rest and clean up before dinner. Julian tried repeatedly to get Jane's attention, but she seemed determined to ignore him, and there wasn't much he could do without making a spectacle of himself.

Later that evening, Julian found himself seated next to Jane at the dining room table, which wasn't surprising, since they were the odd ones out. "How are you?" he asked softly when he sat down beside her, glad to finally have her to himself at least somewhat.

"It was a long trip," she replied remotely. "I'm still feeling a bit tired."

"I hate traveling by coach," he agreed. "I'd much prefer to ride."

Jane sighed. "Well, women don't have that luxury."

He frowned, knowing she was right. "You're a wonderful rider," he said, remembering carefree summer days when the two of them had ridden through the woods that crisscrossed their families' estates. "Do you find the opportunity to do so in the city?"

She shook her head, not meeting his eyes. "No, I'm afraid not. I only own two carriage horses, neither of which is a very good mount."

He found that incredibly sad. "Well, I own a lovely bay mare you'd probably love. Perhaps once we return to London, we can go for a ride through the park."

Eagerness flickered in her eyes for just a moment before she ruthlessly banked it. "Do you really think there's a need for us to continue to see each other, once the wedding is over?"

Feeling as though he'd been punched in the gut, he sank back into his chair. "Need? Perhaps not. But I'd *like* to continue to see you, Jane. How am I supposed to prove myself to you, if you don't give me the opportunity?"

She sighed, pressing her hand to her temple as though she suffered a megrim. "I'm sorry. That was unnecessarily rude of me. I just keep thinking that this has all been a lark for you, that you'll lose interest once we're not forced into close proximity."

Though he knew she had every reason to think poorly of him, he still felt stung by her lack of faith. Since he'd told her he wanted to court her, she'd given him very little reason to believe that was what she wanted. He very greatly feared that once Michael and Emma were wed, they would indeed drift apart again.

"What must I do?" he asked her once again. "I truly do want to prove myself to you."

She finally met his gaze, allowing him to see the seething emotion she'd been trying so hard to conceal. "You hurt me," she whispered. "Do you think it's easy for me to forget that? To trust you again?"

"No," he said softly, aware that Natalia, who was Jane's cousin, was staring at them with obvious concern from across the table. "But I also know that you still care for me. If you didn't, you wouldn't be talking to me at all."

She gave a low, bitter laugh. "You think you know me so well. But I'm not the sweet young girl you once knew. I'm stronger now. I've had to be."

Before he could say more, Natalia cleared her throat. "I'm so glad you're here, Jane! It's been far too long since we saw each other. We must catch up."

He didn't know how much of their whispered conversation Jane's cousin had heard, but she'd obviously decided that Julian was bothering Jane and had decided to take matters into her own hands. Knowing his opportunity to speak to Jane privately had passed, he reluctantly turned his attention to the rest of the table as Jane and Natalia continued to talk.

Once again, he noticed that Dylan seemed upset or nervous about something, which was very unlike him. Dylan generally had a carefree attitude that Julian had always appreciated, which was probably why they'd become such good friends in school. Julian had been drawn to Dylan's sunny disposition the way he'd been drawn to Jane's.

As soon as dinner was over and the group filtered into the parlor, Julian cornered his old friend near the piano. "How's married life?" Julian asked, hoping that Natalia wasn't behind Dylan's brooding. He needed to believe that his friend was still as happy in his marriage as he'd seemed on his wedding day.

Dylan gave a quick grin, setting Julian's mind at ease. "Wonderful. Natalia and I are settling in well at Aldabaran."

Dylan had only recently found out that he'd been left an estate in Scotland by his late maternal grandfather. His father had kept it from him, for no reason that Julian could see other than pure spitefulness. The Earl of Warren had treated his second son as poorly as Julian's own father had treated Ethan.

"You seem distracted," Julian observed, deciding to cut to the chase. "Is something wrong?"

Dylan glanced at Michael. "I have something I need to tell Michael. Something I know is going to hurt him. Natalia convinced me to wait until after the wedding, and I know she's right, but it's eating at me. I've held it inside for too long already."

Julian frowned. "Perhaps you should tell me then."

Dylan gave a short laugh. "Maybe it would help me to get your opinion on the matter. Perhaps you can tell me whether you think I should tell Michael at all."

"Of course," Julian agreed readily, a bad feeling taking root in the pit of his stomach. Because he had no real relationship with his own brother, he'd always thought of Dylan and Michael as his family. He cared deeply for them both and would hate to see either of them hurt.

Dylan glanced around the room once more, making sure that everyone else seemed to be occupied in their own conversations, and led Julian a little farther away from the rest, toward the window. "When I arrived at Aldabaran, I found out that the Earl of Warren is not my true father," he admitted quietly. "My mother had an affair with her father's groom, a man named Patrick MacPherson."

Julian's eyes widened in surprise. "That must have been very shocking. I'm terribly sorry."

Dylan shook his head. "Don't be. I was actually very pleased by the revelation. Patrick is a wonderful man, and he's become the father I always wanted. I'm only sorry that I didn't know the truth much sooner."

When Julian thought of all the pain and heartache the earl had put Dylan through, he saw how it must be a relief to know that the old bastard wasn't actually his father. He'd obviously been making Dylan pay all these years for his mother's betrayal. No wonder Michael found it so hard to trust women.

"I think Michael already knows that your mother was unfaithful," Julian told Dylan, remembering the conversation they'd had the night Michael had met Emma. "I don't think he'll find this too surprising."

Dylan sighed pensively. "I'm sure it wouldn't bother him that much, if that's all I had to tell him." He glanced across the room at his brother, who was staring their way, obviously wondering what they were talking about. Lowering his voice, Dylan continued, "When I arrived in Scotland, I started having terrible nightmares. After I found out about Patrick, I realized that the dreams were actually memories."

"What did you remember?" Julian asked quietly, his heart aching for his friends.

"When I was seven, my mother and I went to spend the summer in Scotland. Michael stayed in London with his father. The earl had paid one of the servants to report back to him about my mother. Apparently, Warren found out that my mother and Patrick were having an affair, and he came up to Scotland to confront her." Dylan swallowed and shook his head. "They got into a fight out by the cliffs, and I saw him push her to her death."

"Dear God," Julian whispered, reaching out to squeeze his friend's shoulder.

"Patrick says I ran away, hid in the smuggler's caves below the castle. It took them days to find me, and I never spoke of it afterward. I think I somehow managed to block it out. But returning to Scotland finally brought all those memories back."

"I'm surprised you haven't killed the old bastard." Julian released his friend's shoulder and glanced back at Michael. "But you're right. This will destroy Michael."

Dylan nodded, his eyes deeply troubled. "Trust me, I'd like nothing more than to kill Warren. But I've got too much to lose now." He nodded slightly in Natalia's direction. "I've decided to leave Warren's punishment up to Michael. He is the one who will suffer most if there is a scandal."

"An earl accused as a murderer? That will be difficult to prove." Julian had no doubt that Dylan was telling the truth, but he knew how hard it would be to convict someone like Warren of such a thing. Especially since Dylan had been a child when he'd witnessed it, and the earl had already gotten away with it for so long. He sighed. "Well, I think Natalia is right. You should wait to tell him until after the wedding. He and Emma have enough problems to deal with already."

"I know you're right," Dylan said. "This has just been eating at me for so long. I know it's always bothered Michael that Warren was so cruel to me. I think perhaps it will ease his mind a bit to know there was a reason for it, that I'm not Warren's child at all."

"Perhaps," Julian said doubtfully. "But he'll also have to confront the fact that his father murdered his mother."

Dylan rubbed his forehead as though he had a sudden headache. "That's true. I'm obviously not thinking clearly. I don't want to hurt Michael. It just infuriates me, you know? To think that he's gotten away with it all these years."

"I understand." Turning, Julian went over to the sideboard and poured them both a glass of brandy, then handed one to Dylan. "But this is a happy occasion. Let's help Michael and Emma celebrate their marriage tonight. We'll worry about the rest tomorrow."

However, as they turned back to the rest of the group, he feared what Dylan's revelations would mean for Michael.

Chapter Seven

Jane couldn't sleep.

The journey to Sherbourne Hall for Emma and Michael's wedding had seemed to take forever, and once she'd arrived, she'd been forced into close quarters with Julian once again. Dinner had been excruciating, with Michael's brother and Jane's cousin Natalia so obviously in love, and Michael and Emma unable to keep their eyes off each other despite the tension between them. She and Julian had been paired up, and she couldn't help thinking how it might be if she'd accepted his proposal and they could be a couple in truth. She'd tried to remain distant this evening, but she had to admit that his sweetness was wearing her down.

The mere fact that Julian was in the room next door made it impossible to close her eyes. If she did, she'd be too tempted to picture him lying in his bed, his magnificent body naked beneath the crisp white sheets.

With a soul-deep sigh, she flung away her blankets and paced the room with growing agitation. Thank God Emma and Michael were finally getting married tomorrow. Once her obligations to the young American were over, she could return home and be spared the constant temptation of Julian's arms.

Why did he have to be so heartbreakingly handsome? He shouldn't speak of things such as love and second chances. She was far too susceptible to his sweet seductive words and smoldering glances.

It wasn't fair.

She desperately wanted to believe he still loved her and wanted her to become his wife.

Her heart begged her to take the risk, but she knew even if he truly wanted her now, it would be a fleeting thing. Once he'd had his fill, he would move on, as he'd done before. Then she'd be left alone in their shell of a marriage, trying to keep up the pretense while her heart shattered.

Still, she couldn't stop thinking of Emma and Michael's passionate embrace, couldn't stop wishing she'd allowed Julian to take such liberties all those years ago. What would it have mattered? What good was her virginity to her now?

She didn't want to die a shriveled-up old prune, having never known what it was like to make love to a man.

Hugging her arms to her chest to fend off a sudden chill, she stared at her mirrored reflection.

"You're too lovely to be a spinster."

Julian's words whispered through her mind, and a new resolve sparked to life within her. Why shouldn't she go to him, now, before the ravages of age caught up to her? Why shouldn't she have one beautiful memory to keep her warm during all the long lonely nights to come?

If she asked him to make love to her, made it clear she had no intention of demanding anything more than a single night of pleasure, he'd probably be relieved. He'd laugh that soft sexy laugh and offer to teach her everything she'd ever wanted to know.

But could she bear that? To know he'd never really wanted anything more?

Yes. She could bear that, and more. Better one lovely evening than a marriage filled with lies and deceit.

Wrapping herself in the heavy flannel robe from the foot of the bed, she slipped out the door. She feared if she paused for more than one second, she'd lose her nerve.

She'd never done anything this daring in her entire life.

Oh, how she wished she had Emma's courage and sense of adventure. If she did, she'd wear purple silk instead of white flannel, and she'd flirt shamelessly instead of tripping over her tongue or hurling waspish insults.

Biting her lip, she lifted her hand to knock on Julian's door, then thought better of it. She couldn't stand here and wait for him to answer. Someone could come along at any moment.

But she'd ventured too far to turn back now, so she gathered her nerve, turned the knob, and slipped inside. Breathing erratically, she sagged against the wall and waited for her eyes to grow accustomed to the dark.

Oh, this was a bad, bad idea. He was already asleep, and he probably wouldn't appreciate her barging in on him like this even if he wasn't.

"Who's there?"

Julian's raspy, sleepy voice startled her. She shrank even closer to the wall and wished the floor would open up and swallow her. She couldn't go through with this. But she didn't know whether to leave or simply remain quiet until he fell asleep again.

The bedclothes rustled, and then he moved toward her through the darkness with unerring accuracy. "Who's there?" This time, his voice sounded dark with menace. "Identify yourself."

Before she could draw breath to answer, he slammed her against the wall with the full weight of his large body. Her breath escaped in a terrified rush as the cold press of steel bit at the tender skin of her throat.

She made a soft sound of distress, dizzy with fear, but with even that small movement, the blade pricked her. "Julian. Please. It's me, Jane."

Immediately, he released her. "Jane?" His voice was hoarse with sleep and confusion. "What the hell are you doing here?"

She shook her head, then realized he couldn't see her in the dark. "I don't know," she whispered, fighting an overwhelming urge to cry. This wasn't going at all the way she planned. "I just wanted to see you."

"You wanted to see me?" He repeated her words slowly, as though he feared he hadn't understood them. "I must be dreaming."

"You're not dreaming." As she spoke, she groped behind her for the doorknob. "But this was a mistake. I never should have come."

Finding what she sought, she pulled the door open, only to freeze as light spilled into the room from the hallway beyond. Her earlier suspicions were illuminated in stunning, beautiful detail.

I was right. He sleeps in the nude.

Her gaze swept over his body, taking in every hard, muscular detail. She couldn't have looked away if her life depended on it. In fact, she feared she was the one dreaming.

But even in her wildest fantasies, she'd never imagined *this*.

His black hair was mussed and fell in soft waves over his forehead, framing his dark eyes. His chest was powerfully chiseled, covered by a mat of curly dark hair that narrowed to trail down his lean stomach. She dared to let her gaze drop even farther, then swallowed dryly at what she saw.

"I really should go," she repeated, a bit desperate. "I'm sorry for disturbing you."

Julian stepped forward, barring her exit. "Don't leave." He lifted a large warm hand and tenderly cupped her cheek. Then he paused, staring down at her throat. "I've cut you."

"It's all right. It doesn't hurt."

"You're bleeding." Shutting the door, he took her hand and drew her across the room, dangerously near the bed. "Wait here."

The was some rustling and a low curse, and after a moment, an oil lamp flared to life, casting a small island of light in the darkness. With some regret, she noticed he'd wrapped a crisp white sheet around his lean hips.

Cutting off a corner with his knife, he dipped the ragged piece of fabric into a glass of brandy on the nightstand beside his rumpled bed.

"This might sting." Moving closer, he dabbed gently at the small cut. "God, Jane. I'm so sorry."

"It's all right," she assured him. "This was my fault entirely."

"Don't be ridiculous."

Her eyelids fluttered shut at his tender touch, and she breathed deeply, inhaling Julian's clean warm scent. She felt so strange. Her limbs seemed heavy, as though she couldn't have moved even if she'd wanted to.

"There." At last, he lowered the damp cloth. "I think you'll live."

Reluctantly, she opened her eyes and found him staring down at her, his beautiful mouth just inches from hers. "I really should go."

"No."

His sharp tone startled her. She took a step back, but he immediately gentled. "Please, Jane. Stay for a while. Tell me why you came."

She stared at him, unsure how to go about getting what she wanted. With a nervous swallow, she pulled her robe tighter around her waist.

This was definitely not how Emma would have handled the situation. Dropping her gaze to the middle of his broad chest, to the soft-looking patch of dark hair that grew between his flat male nipples, she struggled to find the right words.

"I've been thinking about what you said the other day. And I've come to a decision."

"You have?" With a glad cry, he swung her up in his arms and cradled her against his chest. "Thank God," he whispered, covering her face with a tender storm of kisses. "I thought you'd never forgive me. I thought I'd live the rest of my life without ever holding you in my arms again."

Stunned by his erroneous assumption of her motives and overwhelmed by his kisses, Jane couldn't find the breath to contradict him. He turned and lowered her to the bed, then followed her down, pressing her deep into the mattress with the heat and weight of his lean body. "I've been such a fool." He met her gaze earnestly, tracing her cheek with one gentle fingertip. "But I swear I'll make it up to you."

She knew he thought she was agreeing to marry him, but she was so enraptured by his tenderness she couldn't bring herself to shatter the illusion. Feeling quite daring, she brushed a few strands of silky black hair out of his eyes and lifted her mouth to his.

With a soft groan, he transformed her chaste kiss into a scorching brand of possession. She gasped as his tongue captured hers, flooding her senses with a taste of brandy.

He'd kissed her before, years ago, but she'd forgotten how quickly passion could build. Restless, she ran her hands over his hair and the warmth of his skin, trying to get closer.

He nudged her clenched thighs apart with one knee. His scalding erection rubbed insistently against her core, and the resulting pleasure was nearly more than she could bear.

Shuddering, he broke the kiss and stared down at her. His chest heaved as though he'd run a great distance. "Tell me you love me. Please, Jane. I need to hear the words."

Tell me you love me. As she looked into his beautiful, passion-drawn face, she knew she always had. She always would.

Tears filled her eyes, and she tried to drive them back. "Let's not talk. Don't spoil it."

"Spoil it?" Julian resisted her clinging arms and pinned her with an incredulous look. "What's going on? Why the hell did you come here tonight if you don't love me?"

"I'm offering you my body. Isn't that enough?"

He stared at her for a long moment, then rolled away and sat on the edge of the bed. Trembling, she sat up and drew her knees to her chest as she stared at the rigid line of his back.

"Let me see if I've got this straight," he said, after an endless moment of silence. "You don't love me; you just want to fuck me?"

She flinched at the ugly word but refused to let him make her feel bad about this. He was the one who had walked away. He'd broken her heart. How dare he expect her to be foolish enough to trust him again?

"I can't marry you," she told him, struggling not to give in to her tears. "I can't give my heart to you again."

He leaned forward, bracing his elbows on his knees as he buried his face in his hands. "I don't want just one night in your bed, Jane. I want all of you. I want us to have what Dylan and Natalia have."

She inched toward him and gently caressed his shoulder. "I want that, too. But surely, you see how impossible it is. I couldn't hold your love when we were young, and I doubt anything has changed. You see your friends marrying, and you want to have that kind of closeness. But how can we, when you don't even know me?"

"I know you. You're the only one besides Dylan and Michael who has ever given a damn about me."

She sighed. "You want me to love you, but I don't think you're capable of loving me in return. I can't live like that. I can't spend the rest of my life worrying that you're with another woman every time you walk out the door."

"It wouldn't be like that," he whispered. "I would never do that to you."

She wanted to believe him. She wanted it with every fiber of her being. But she couldn't. She knew him too well.

"I want you. Can't it be as easy as that? Just give me tonight, Julian. You know that's all you really want. Don't make me live the rest of my life without ever knowing passion." Emboldened by desperation, she let her hand drift down to rest on the straining bulge of his manhood, which pressed against the thin sheet.

He caught his breath, and the rigid shaft of flash leapt against her hand. "What the hell do you think you're doing? Don't you know you're playing with fire?"

Before she could answer, he closed his eyes and covered her hand with his. Then he moved her hand again. One long, slow stroke. His entire body shuddered, and he let out a low sound of what she hoped was pleasure but could just as easily have been pain.

That was all he allowed himself before he firmly thrust her away.

"I do love you," he told her, his voice shaking with frustration. "But I've never been so insulted in my life. I offer you marriage, and you tell me you'd rather become my whore."

"Julian, please..." She tried to touch him again, but he surged to his feet.

"Get out." He glared at her as though the mere sight of her disgusted him. "Right now."

She stared at him for one long minute, her heart breaking anew as she realized how terribly she'd wronged him. She *had* insulted him. From the look in his eyes, she didn't think he'd ever forgive or forget this. "I'm sorry," she whispered. Then she fled.

LONG AFTER JANE LEFT, passion still surged through Julian.

He sprawled across his bed on his back, glad for the chill in the air, though it seemed to be doing little to cool his aching erection.

"Bloody hell!" he cursed violently, reaching for the brandy on his nightstand and downing it in one gulp. He still couldn't believe she'd come to him, wanting nothing more than sex, throwing his claims of love in his face, refusing to trust him, refusing to *love* him.

He couldn't believe he'd let her go. She'd felt so good beneath him, her vanilla and lavender scent enveloping him, kissing him so sweetly he'd thought he'd died and gone to heaven. He'd thought that she'd forgiven him and had briefly envisioned that they'd manage to build a life together.

How had he become such a lovesick fool?

He should have taken her up on her offer. Maybe she was right and once he'd had her, he'd grow bored and want to move on.

He covered his face with a pillow, muffling a groan of frustration. Because he knew that wasn't true. He'd been with enough women to know the difference between love and sex. And with every encounter he had with Jane, he was more convinced that if she'd just give him a second chance, he could show her more love than she'd ever imagined.

But after Michael and Emma were married tomorrow, he'd no longer be seeing her on a regular basis. And without their friends pushing them together time and again, he had no idea how to continue his suit. Should he even try? How could he bear it if she rejected him again?

Chapter Eight

Jane glanced over her shoulder at the darkened street, shifting nervously as she waited for one of Julian's servants to open his front door. The hour was late, and she'd arrived unescorted. She'd be ruined if anyone saw her here.

The anxious energy coursing through her reminded her of last week, when she had gone to Julian's bedroom at Sherbourne Hall. This time, however, her purpose was not seduction.

Another interminable minute passed, but finally, the door opened, creaking on its hinges. The dour-faced butler stared at her, obviously aghast. "May I help you, madam?"

Jane's face grew hot. She knew how this must look and could only hope Julian's staff would be discreet. "I need to speak with Lord Basingstoke. Immediately."

The man stiffened with disapproval. "Who shall I say is calling?"

"Lady Jane Bennett," she answered, then wondered if Julian would receive her after the way they'd parted. "Tell him it's an emergency."

"Very well." The butler stepped aside to let her in, then showed her to the receiving room. "I'll see if Lord Basingstoke is in."

Jane perched on the edge of the nearest chair. Her pulse thundered in her ears. What would she do if Julian *wasn't* in? In all likelihood, he was in the arms of another woman at this very moment. Perhaps he even had a woman here, and that was why the butler seemed so flustered. She didn't know what she'd do if the butler tried to send her away, but she'd have to think of something.

She couldn't leave here until she'd spoken to Julian.

Long moments passed, but at last, footsteps echoed in the hall. She took a deep breath, preparing herself, then let it out in a rush of relief when Julian entered the room.

He'd obviously been getting ready for bed, as he wore only a loose white linen shirt and buff trousers. Her gaze dropped to the shocking elegance of his long bare feet.

"So." He leaned against the door frame, a mocking expression on his saturnine face. "Have you come to try your hand at seducing me again? Perhaps, this time, I'll let you."

He was in a dark, dangerous mood. She thanked God she hadn't come here for herself. He would never believe how sorry she was for hurting him.

"I thought you might want to know that your friend, Michael, needs you. He stands accused of murdering the Earl of Warren."

"My God." Julian pushed away from the wall, his entire manner changing from anger to concern. "Are you quite certain? How did you learn of this?"

"My lady's maid." Jane was glad to provide him with what little information she had. "She's been seeing one of the earl's grooms, and the young man raced over to spread the news right after it happened."

Julian raked one hand through his dark hair. "Bloody hell, I knew I shouldn't have let him confront the bastard on his own." For a moment, he seemed stunned into immobility but then he shook himself. "I have to go sort this out."

His confidence filled her with relief. She didn't know what had happened, but she couldn't imagine Michael hurting anyone, especially his father. There had to be some sort of mistake.

If anyone could help, it would be Julian.

Muttering under his breath, Julian turned back the way he'd come. Then he stopped abruptly and gave her a grateful glance over his shoulder. "Thank you, Jane. I know it couldn't have been easy for you to come here tonight."

She smiled at him through a veil of tears. "Go help your friend, Julian. And then, perhaps, when this is over, we can talk?"

He gave her a searching glance, then returned her wry smile. "Perhaps."

He left the room, and she allowed the butler to see her back to the door. As her carriage started toward home, sudden tears filled her eyes. He'd been kind to her, when she had very much feared that he'd be cold and cutting.

After what she'd done to him at Sherbourne Hall, he had every right to be angry with her. That next day, during Emma and Michael's wedding, he'd been polite but distant, talking to her only when he had to but overall doing his best to avoid her.

During the long, lonely trip back to London, she'd had plenty of time to think about everything that had happened between her and Julian, from their first kiss to the passionate encounter at Sherbourne Hall. As she'd obsessively dissected everything she knew about the man Julian had become, the more convinced she'd become that he'd grown up, that he was no longer the reckless boy he'd once been.

He'd done everything he could to try and apologize for his past actions. He'd reached out to her time and again, and she'd done nothing but slap his hand away. Shame over her actions the night she'd gone to his room had overwhelmed her. He'd said he loved her, and she didn't think he'd faked the look of hurt and betrayal in his eyes.

If all he'd really wanted was to have his way with her, he would have done so. The fact that he'd turned her away had proven that he'd changed more than anything else possibly could have.

But now that she believed him, she greatly feared that it was too late.

All she could hope for was that he truly did come to find her once he'd done what he could to help Michael.

DURING THE NEXT FEW days, Julian put all his energy into helping Michael extricate himself from the dangerous accusations he faced regarding his father's death. He'd ridden hard for Sherbourne Hall to tell Emma what had happened, then went to tell Dylan as well. Since he knew what Dylan had told Michael about their mother's death, he'd immediately assumed that Michael truly had killed his father, determined to make him pay for his past crimes. However, Michael had claimed that the earl had committed suicide when he'd confronted him with his crimes, preferring death to scandal and prison.

Julian hadn't believed him, but he also hadn't cared. He'd been determined to stand by his friend, to lend his support, time, money, and reputation to see that Michael got out of this mess, no matter what he'd done.

He'd been ashamed when both Emma and Dylan had immediately believed in Michael's innocence. Why hadn't he? He'd assumed the worst, and he realized that he'd lived his entire life that way.

He'd blamed Ethan for Nathanial and Elizabeth's deaths, parroting his angry, grief-stricken parents. He'd allowed that to rob him of his little brother's love, of the only family he had left. Then he'd run away from Jane's love as well, too afraid to risk his heart again.

He couldn't help thinking that Jane had taken a risk herself, coming to tell him what had happened to Michael. Now that everything had settled down, could he do any less? Yes, she might refuse him again, but if he didn't even try then he had only himself to blame for the long lonely years to come.

Chapter Nine

A week after going to Julian's home, Jane walked down the hall toward her bedroom, dreading the thought of another long lonely night. The big old house seemed far too empty now that Emma was gone.

Although it was still early, she'd chosen to retire to her room with a book. Perhaps, lost in the pages, she could banish her melancholy. She wanted to pretend, if only for a little while, that she was someone else, someone other than a forgotten spinster who had nothing to look forward to but an eternity of her own company.

Entering her room, Jane put her book down on a nearby table and bent to light the lamp next to her favorite reading chair.

"Hello, Jane."

Startled, she shrieked and whirled toward the source of the deep male voice... only to find Julian lounging in the middle of her large pedestal bed.

"How did you get in here?" She stared at him in stunned surprise. Her heart hammered erratically in her chest, the sudden fear giving way to desperate hope.

"Through the window." His smile was wicked. "Did you think you were the only one adept at sneaking into people's bedrooms at night?"

"I suppose not. I just wasn't expecting you." Now *that* was the understatement of the year.

Even after the tentative truce they'd reached the night she'd told him of Michael's arrest, she'd never dreamed he'd seek her out.

Greedily, she drank in the sight of him, so handsome, his black hair and clothes a stark contrast to the snowy white counterpane. Holding her gaze, he came to a sitting position and dropped his long legs off the side of the bed.

"You said we should talk." He shrugged. "I thought I'd raise a few eyebrows by knocking on your front door at this time of night."

She took a few hesitant steps in his direction and wondered if she looked as terrible as she feared. Her hair was scraped up in an unflattering bun, and her serviceable brown dress did nothing for her pale complexion.

"How is Michael? Did you get a chance to speak to him?" She truly did want to know how their mutual friend fared, but she was stalling, terrified that she'd misinterpreted the reason for his unexpected visit.

"I've seen him several times." He sighed and loosened his cravat, exposing the strong column of his throat to her interested gaze. "He claims the earl committed suicide. At first, I didn't believe him. You see, I know what they argued about. Michael found out that the son of a bitch murdered his mother all those years ago."

"Poor Michael," Jane blurted, stunned. "It must've been terrible for him to confront his father with such knowledge. But if he says the earl killed himself, then I'm certain that's what happened."

"Apparently, you have more faith in my friend than I do. I feel like the worst sort of ass for not believing him all along."

"Don't be so hard on yourself. The important thing is that you were willing to stand by him, even though you thought he was guilty."

"Well, at least I managed to do one thing right. I rallied a rather formidable defense. I alerted Emma and Dylan of Michael's predicament, even though he begged me not to. They are both standing steadfastly by his side, and Emma's father has enlisted the help of an entire retinue of barristers."

"You don't think he'll be convicted of murder, do you?" Jane shuddered at the thought.

Julian shook his head. "I doubt it. There will be quite a scandal. People will whisper behind his back for years to come. But I doubt anything else will come of it. Right or wrong, his position will protect him."

"That's good. I've been sick with worry ever since I heard what happened." She took a deep breath. "Is that why you came here tonight? To talk about Michael?"

Julian shot her an irritated glance. "Do you really think that's the only reason I'm here?"

She stared across the distance that separated them, knowing her heart was in her eyes. "I hope not. But I wouldn't blame you if it was."

"Come sit beside me. I don't intend to spend the rest of the evening shouting at you from across the room."

The rest of the evening? That was encouraging.

She realized how foolish she must look, frozen in place in the middle of her bedroom. After all, she'd been waiting for this chance her entire life. She climbed up on the bed and gingerly sat on the very edge.

"I won't bite." A short burst of exasperated laughter escaped Julian's lips. He gave her a devilish grin. "At least, not unless you want me to."

She stared at him, surprised by the sexual innuendo and uncertain how to react.

He sighed, and his knee brushed her hip with startling intimacy. "I'm here, sweetheart, against all my better judgment." He met her gaze with heartbreaking directness. "You know how I feel. The next move is up to you."

She bit her lip, overwhelmed by his willingness to give her a second chance. It couldn't have been easy for him, given the way she'd treated him.

It was time for her to put her heart on the line—to take a chance and reach for the love she'd always dreamed of. It was better to risk fresh heartbreak than spend the rest of her life alone and filled with regret.

Hesitantly, she reached for his hand.

He twined his fingertips with hers, and a shimmering warmth shot up her arm. He squeezed gently, as if to give her courage.

Smiling through a sudden sheen of tears, she leaned forward and pressed her lips against his smooth warm cheek. "I've been such a fool. I wanted to believe you cared for me. Truly, I did. It just seems so impossible that someone like you could love someone like me."

"Someone like you?" He cupped her chin with his other hand and forced her to look at him. "What the devil do you mean by that?"

She shrugged, embarrassed heat rushing to her cheeks. "I'm nobody. A plain, dried-up old spinster. I lead such a quiet boring life. It's difficult for me to believe you could ever be happy sharing it."

"As long as you're cataloging your faults, don't forget blind and misguided." Julian pulled her into his lap and hugged her fiercely. "Ah, Jane. You're the most beautiful, exciting creature I've ever known. There are a thousand things I want to tell you, a million questions I want to ask. I could never grow tired of you. Not in a dozen lifetimes."

She clung to him, stunned by the truth she heard in his words. His heartfelt speech transformed her, cracked the safe little cocoon of her spinsterhood.

Spreading her newfound wings, she somehow found the strength to make a declaration of her own. She pulled back, so she could see the expression in his dark eyes. "I love you, Julian. I never stopped. Not even for a moment."

"Oh, sweetheart. I love you, too. More than I ever thought possible." A tremor coursed through his big lean body. "Can you ever forgive me for leaving you? For not being there when you needed me?"

"I've already forgiven you." Tears swam across her vision and obscured his beautiful face. She wasn't sure if they were tears of happiness or if she was mourning all the lost years. "Just promise me you'll never leave me again. I couldn't bear it."

"I'm never going to let you go." His arms tightened around her. "When we were young, it came so easily. I didn't recognize it for the precious gift it was. Believe me, if I'd known you were the only one who'd ever make me feel that way, I never would have walked away."

"Oh, Julian." She couldn't hold the past against him any longer. She knew how lost he'd been back then, confused and heartbroken over the loss of his family. He'd been running, just as she had been when he came back into her life.

Satisfied they'd worked things out for now, she pressed her mouth to his and kissed him with all the passion in her lonely soul.

For a moment, he remained passive in her embrace, allowing her to leisurely explore his beautiful lips. Then, with a deep groan, he deepened the kiss, devouring her with his turbulent need.

She fell into the kiss with complete abandon, clinging to his broad chest as all of her fears and doubts faded away and only love and passion remained. Before long, kisses were not enough, and they began to fumble with each other's clothes. She worked on his cravat as he undid her buttons, and then suddenly, they were skin to skin, her bare breasts pressed against his chest.

His hands drifted gently over her curves, and she ran her hands over him as well, stunned by his smooth heated skin, the swells of his muscles, and the flat ridges of his stomach. He pressed her down onto the bed, then began to kiss her everywhere his hands had been.

She sighed and sank back into the mattress, her hands falling to her sides as she just let herself enjoy it. She'd waited a lifetime to be touched this way by this man. But not even in her wildest dreams could she have imagined such pleasure. She felt as though she was melting, a fire burning in the pit of her stomach, making her yearn for something more, something she couldn't even name.

He drew back a bit and stared down at her, his dark eyes worshipful. "You're so beautiful," he whispered. "I knew you would be."

His words made her feel beautiful, and she was stunned by how unselfconscious she was to be naked with him. She thought he was beautiful, too, but she didn't say it. She was beyond words as his fingertips drifted down the soft curve of her belly and delved gently between her thighs.

She gasped, and he caught the sound with his lips, kissing her again as he gently explored her in ways she'd never imagined. Pleasure began to build within her, and she clutched at him, unsure what exactly was happening but loving every moment of it. He found the sweetest spot and focused his attention there until she was trembling and gasping into his mouth.

Just when she was sure she couldn't take the pleasure any longer, he pressed his fingertip inside her, and she suddenly convulsed around him, crying out in surprised delight.

"Ah, sweetheart," he breathed, holding her tightly against him as she slowly came back to herself. "I love to give you pleasure."

She laughed softly, still stunned and breathless. "That was amazing."

"Good," he whispered, kissing her forehead with incredible tenderness.

Even though she was very inexperienced when it came to lovemaking, she knew that there was more. She gathered her courage and let her hand trail down his chest and lower, gliding down the soft arrow of hair until her knuckles brushed against the hard, hot length of him. He jerked and let out a soft appreciative sigh.

"Is this all right?" she asked. "May I touch you?"

"Yes, please," he whispered, rolling on his back and gazing at her with hooded eyes.

She pushed up on one elbow and gazed down at him, stunned by his beauty. She still couldn't believe that he was here, in her bed, and she was free to touch him however she wanted. Biting her lip, she reached out and lightly traced her hand down his body from chest to that huge hard part of him. It felt silky smooth and hot in her palm, and he covered her hand with his own, showing her how to stroke him, how to give him the same sort of pleasure he'd given her.

For endless moments she touched him, learning all the secrets of his male body, so caught up in his heat and strength and beauty that she couldn't be embarrassed or ashamed. Then, suddenly, he groaned and rolled them again.

He stared down at her, so much love and passion in his eyes she wondered how she'd ever doubted him. "I want to make love to you. Are you ready for that, Jane?"

She cupped his cheek, knowing that they'd gone too far to turn back now. She had to put her trust him, make this leap of faith. "Yes," she whispered. "I'm yours, Julian. I've always been yours."

"Mine," he whispered, giving her another sweet kiss before pressing his knee between her thighs, coaxing her to spread her legs so that he could lay between them. She felt his hardness press against her core, and she couldn't help but surge against him, wanting to be even closer.

He reached between them, and then he was pressing deeper, filling her. He suddenly thrust forward and there was a bright, hot moment of pain that made her cry out, but then he was inside her and the pain quickly faded, leaving only pleasure.

"Are you all right?" he asked, staring down at her, his body trembling with the need to hold back. "Did I hurt you?"

"It's all right," she assured him, rubbing her hands up and down his back. "It only hurt for a moment."

He smiled, then flexed his hips again, and this time, there was only a slight discomfort. A few strokes more, and she started to feel that building pressure again. She clung to him as the storm burst inside her once more, and she sobbed his name as she gave into it.

A few moments later, he seemed caught up in a storm of his own. He cried out, too, and then he stiffened and collapsed atop her.

She cradled him to her, feeling more at peace than she'd ever been in her life. No matter what happened, she would not go to her grave as a virgin, completely untouched and unloved. She'd made love to the man she'd cared for all her life, and she couldn't regret it.

For a long time, they just drifted in the pleasant aftermath, holding each other tightly. Finally, he broke away, staring down at her, his dark eyes fierce. "Say you'll marry me, Jane. The uncertainty is killing me."

"Of course, I'll marry you," she declared, laughing through her tears. "It's all I've ever wanted."

Relief flooded his features, and he hugged her tight. "Thank you," he breathed, his face buried in her hair. "Forgive me for throwing the miracle of us away when I was young and stupid. I promise you I'll spend the rest of my life treating you like the rare and perfect treasure that you are."

"I'll hold you to that," she whispered, tears of happiness stinging her eyes. "And I'll never take you for granted either."

They drifted in pleasant silence for a long time more, and Jane was more than happy to simply drift off in his arms. But he sighed, kissed her forehead, and reluctantly set her away.

"I must go," he said. "I don't want to risk anyone finding me here."

"I have a very small staff," she protested. "No one will come until morning."

He pushed himself to a sitting position and smiled. "I'm afraid if I fall asleep in your bed, I'll never want to leave it."

She pouted a bit. "I don't think I care if we're caught. We're to be married. Does it really matter?"

"Of course, it matters." He gave her a chiding glance before standing up and beginning to dress. "I want to do this right. I want you to have an engagement party, a big wedding, everything that you deserve. The last thing I want is any rumors or ugliness to ruin it."

She bit her lip, happiness swelling within her. He really had changed, and though she wished for nothing more than for him to stay, she knew he was right. She loved that he was protecting her reputation, and she decided to let him do everything he'd said for her. She sensed he needed to.

Then a horrible thought occurred to her. "Does this mean that we have to wait until we are wed to be together like this again?" She now understood completely why Michael and Emma had risked their passionate embrace.

He gave her a sinful smile and came back and dropped a searing kiss on her lips. "We'll find a way," he assured her. "And in a few months, we'll be together every night."

He finished dressing, and then he went back out the window the way he'd come. With a happy sigh, she sank back against her pillow. Earlier this evening, she'd thought that all was lost, that she'd be a spinster forever, untouched and unloved.

But Julian had touched and loved her well, and now the future looked brighter than she'd ever imagined it could be.

Epilogue

Three weeks later...

Julian had always told himself that he didn't need a family, but as he gazed around his drawing room on the night of his engagement party, he realized that over the years, he'd slowly built one of his own. Dylan and Natalia sat on the sofa, their dark heads bent together, her hand resting lightly on the imperceptible rise of her belly where their first child nestled. Michael and Emma were laughing near the fireplace, obviously deeply in love with each other. Michael had been cleared of all charges relating to his father's death, and Julian had never seen his friend so happy.

Best of all, the woman he'd loved most of his life stood beside him, even after everything he'd done. They'd officially announced their engagement to their friends half an hour ago, and they would be wed at Christmastime, at Basingstoke Castle.

This was not the family God had given him, but they were his just the same, and he was grateful for every one of them. His only regret was that Ethan remained half a world away, still convinced that Julian didn't want him in his life.

Something of his sudden melancholy must have shown in his face, because Jane stepped closer, a concerned look in her eyes. "Is something wrong?"

He sighed. "I was just thinking about Ethan. Ever since Harding approached me about bringing him home, I've been trying to think of what I could possibly say that would convince him to do so. I regret what I did to him nearly as much as I regret my actions regarding you."

She grabbed his hand and squeezed it tightly. "You'll never truly be at peace until you reach out to him. I think you should write to him. Tell him you're sorry and ask him if he'll come home for our wedding."

He stared at her, then smiled. "Do you truly think it could be that easy?"

She shrugged. "I can't say what his reaction will be. But all you can do is try. You can apologize and ask him to be a part of your life once again. Even if he refuses, you'll have done what you could to make things right."

Impulsively, he reached out and hugged her tightly, uncaring that everyone in the room could see them. It wasn't as if any of them would be scandalized, and he just really needed to hold this incredible woman for a moment. She'd made his life better than he'd ever thought it could be, and he couldn't wait to make her his bride.

"Thank you," he whispered. "You're absolutely right. All I can do is tell him how very sorry I am and hope that he is as willing to forgive me as you have been."

"You are a good man, Julian," she murmured, pressing her lips tenderly to the curve of his throat, sending a shaft of pure heat through him. "Once he gets to know you again, I'm sure he'll love you as much as I do."

He closed his eyes briefly, treasuring the moment, and then laughed and stepped back. "I'll write to him tonight," he assured her. "And then we'll just have to wait and see what happens."

She gestured around the room. "No matter what happens, you have a lot of people who love you."

He nodded. He'd made many mistakes in his life, but he still had good friends and a good woman to love. "I'm a very lucky man."

She cast a quick glance around to make sure no one was watching them, then gave him a look filled with heated promise. "I'll leave my bedroom window open tonight, if you'd like to be even luckier."

He laughed heartily and hugged her again. His little spinster had finally become the passionate woman he'd always known she could be.

The End

I hope you enjoyed reading Sebastian and Jocelyn's story as much as I enjoyed writing it! If you did, I would greatly appreciate a short review where you purchased it or your favorite book website. Reviews are crucial for any author, and even just a sentence or two can make a huge difference.

You can contact Diana at Diana@dianabold.com

Visit her website at www.dianabold.com

Like her on Facebook for news and freebies

https://www.facebook.com/Dianaboldbooks/

Diana's Bold Beauties | Facebook

Diana is also one of the Brazen Belles, a group of ten similar writers who have a really fun joint FB page! The Brazen Belles | Facebook

Click on the following link to sign up for Diana's newsletter.

Sign up for Diana's Newsletter!

OTHER BOOKS BY DIANA BOLD

VICTORIAN ROMANCE

BRIDES OF SCANDAL SERIES

Gambling on the Duke's Daughter

Marrying the American Heiress

Seducing the Spinster

Finding the Black Orchid

UNMASKING PROMETHEUS SERIES

Masked Intentions

Masked Promises

Masked Desires

Dark Intentions

Dark Promises[1]

Dark Desires

Once a Pirate

Fortune's Gamble

FANTASY ROMANCE

A Knight in Atlantis

WESTERN ROMANCE

LAST CHANCE BRIDES SERIES

One Last Chance

Chance of a Lifetime

Love at Last

The Last Bride

Once a Gunslinger

Once a Mail Order Bride

Once a Bandit

Once an Outlaw

1. https://books2read.com/u/38d8Mr

Diana Bold has been writing since elementary school and never wanted to be anything but a writer. It took longer than she hoped to accomplish that, but she is now the award-winning author of more than thirty historical romances. She lives in the mountains of Southern Colorado with the love of her life, whom she met rather late in life but was worth the wait. When she's not writing, she enjoys traveling and genealogy.

Don't miss out!

Visit the website below and you can sign up to receive emails whenever Diana Bold publishes a new book. There's no charge and no obligation.

https://books2read.com/r/B-A-QJSG-ABEAB

BOOKS 2 READ

Connecting independent readers to independent writers.

Printed in Great Britain
by Amazon

55731009R00058